FAN CAFÉ

SAMANTHA ANN

Edited by PROOF POSITIVE
Cover by KIM CAVRAK
Formatted by GARNET CHRISTIE

DEDICATION

For those who question it, you matter.

HANGUL CHEAT SHEET

Consonants:	Vowels:
ㄱ – g,k	ㅏ – ah
ㄴ – n	ㅐ – ay
ㄷ – d	ㅑ – ya
ㄹ – r,l (say "real" but with an l in the beginning "leal")	ㅒ – yae
ㅁ – m	ㅓ – eo
ㅂ – b	ㅔ – eh
ㅅ – s	ㅕ –yeo
ㅇ – no sound if it starts the word, 'ng' sound if it finishes	ㅗ – o
ㅈ – j	ㅘ –wa
ㅊ – ch	ㅙ –wae
ㅋ – k	ㅚ – oe
ㅌ – t	ㅛ – yo
ㅍ – p	ㅜ – u
ㅎ – h	ㅝ – whoa
ㄲ – gg	ㅞ – we
ㄸ – dd	ㅟ –wi
ㅃ – bb	ㅠ – yu
ㅉ – jj	ㅡ – oo
ㅆ – ss	ㅢ ·ui
	ㅣ – ee
	ㅖ -ye

FAN CAFÉ OST

DU DU DU (English version) – TAN
Fake Happy – Seori
Nice Guy – BOYNEXTDOOR
Unfair(Felix) – Stray Kids
FLY – Gaho
So let's go see the stars – BOYNEXTDOOR
Moonstruck – ENHYPEN
TASTE – JUNNY
Running Through The Night – Seori
Sacrifice – Han Seungwoo
right where you left me - eaJ

CHAPTER ONE

Ther e were only a small number of days Bridgette regretted owning and running a late-night study café. And tonight was one of the biggest.

One of her absolute favorite Korean pop groups, CLAR1T, was in town for two shows. Her best friend, Sophia, had even scored them tickets to both nights. But the first night Bridgette knew would be a busy day at the shop, so she decided to be the responsible adult and work instead. She would still be able to see them the following night.

Somehow being responsible bit her in the ass.

Bridgette's only other employee, the one who was supposed to work the late-night shift so Bridgette could see CLAR1T at their second show in town, called out sick. Making her the only one left to run the shop. She couldn't afford to close for the night, and so she had to text Sophia and tell her to give the ticket to someone else.

Being an adult really did suck sometimes. Instead of seeing the six sexy men of CLAR1T dance, sing, rap, and provide endless amounts of fan service, she was serving coffee to college students who were late-night cramming for exams from one of several colleges in the city. Something she didn't miss.

There she was, sitting at the counter, instead of standing huddled with other CLARvoyants. She called out to the few people in the café that she would be closing up shop in two hours. Most of the students packed up their stuff, grabbing one more cup of coffee and a pastry before exiting. Within a half hour, she was alone. As she waited for some random stragglers to come in for their studying caffeine fix, she pulled her phone out of her apron to scroll through X to see what CLARvoyants were posting about the concert.

Bits of the show began to funnel through her feed, and she got even more excited to see her bias, Minhwa, being his funny 막내* self. And that's when her phone vibrated and a text from Sophia came through.

Sophia: Caught in 4k

A video followed that Bridgette quickly opened. It was Woo Shin, Bridgette's bias wrecker who Sophia was convinced was actually her bias, body rolling as he dropped to his knees and giving the floor a few good pumps before the rest of the boys came running to stop him as the fans screamed and lost their minds. Bridgette had to contain a similar squeal, just in case someone walked in, and covered her large smile as a blush rose to her face.

Sophia was so close to the stage that Bridgette wondered if the staff member Sophia had mentioned having a rather wild time together the previous night, had gotten her a better location. Adding to Bridgette's jealousy of missing the show and possibly meeting this mystery man Sophia had gushed about that morning.

After a half hour of scrolling, she put down her phone to gaze out the window at the city streets. People walked past here and there, peeking in the windows to see if she was actually open, but then proceeded past, probably realizing she wasn't a bar. Suddenly one tall figure peeped in. She couldn't see much of his face, as he had a cap and mask on. After a few seconds, he walked to the door, pulling it open, the jingle of the bells alerting her he was entering.

Bridgette happily greeted him, which only garnered a head nod. She didn't take it personally; people had social anxiety about going

---

* 막내 – maknae - youngest

into restaurants and cafés and having to order. As he came closer to the counter, she realized how tall he really was.

And his shoulders were broad. Very broad.

He was looking at the menu behind her, which allowed her to take in his rather long neck, the muscles taut and his Adam's apple gently bobbing. He had some strands of medium-length gray-blonde hair covering the back of his neck, which was a color she didn't see often on men coming into her shop. She also caught how mesmerizing his dark brown, almost black eyes were as they sparkled under the soft lighting in her café. When he looked down, his eyes disappeared in the shadow of his baseball cap, but she caught sight of a small bun of that same gray-blonde hair poking out the back of the hat.

She shook off the daydreaming of what his whole face looked like and focused on doing her job.

"Do you know what you would like?" She smiled kindly.

"아이스 아메리카노*, please." His accented voice was sweet and gave away the fact that he was Korean. Weirdly that made his hair and mask make sense.

"아아†?" she responded. His eyes went wide, most likely because she was a strawberry-blonde, blue-eyed white girl who knew the Korean slang for an iced Americano.

"네, 감사합니다‡." He dipped his head in gratitude as he pulled out cash to pay.

After handing him his change, Bridgette turned away to make his drink. As the espresso began dripping into the small carafe, she sneakily tried to get a better look at him, but he was very good at keeping his face hidden. That only made her more curious.

She poured the hot espresso over ice, adding water and another small scoop of ice to the cup. Pressing the lid closed, she walked back to hand him the cup and straw.

---

* 아이스 아메리카노 - aiseu amelikano – iced americano

† 아아 – a a – slang for Iced Americano

‡ 네, 감사합니다 - ne, gamsahabnida – yes, thank you.

SAMANTHA ANN

"여기요*." She again gave her brightest customer service smile to get any kind of reaction from the mysterious man. Sadly all she got was another whispered, "감사합니다."

He bowed and walked over to take a seat at one of the two-person tables by the front window. From a backpack she hadn't noticed initially, he pulled out a set of off-white headphones and covered his ears while, similarly to what she had been doing before he walked in, staring out the window to watch people as they walked by.

With that, it was silent, minus the lo-fi playlist she had softly playing in the café. She glanced at the clock on the wall to see there was less than an hour until she closed. While the curious patron sat at the front of the store, she chose to begin her usual end-of-day cleaning around the shop. The young man continued to stare out the window, in his own little world as she wiped the tabletops around him. Whenever she could get a look at him, she noticed his eyes held a sadness that made her wonder if he was going to be okay once he left her café.

She wasn't sure why the worry had hit her so strongly, but as she walked back to the counter to bag up the pastries for her nightly drop at the women's shelter, she caught his reflection on the glass of the display as he let out a long, strong sigh. Grabbing a croissant, she placed it on a plate and strode over to his pensive figure. When she placed it on his table, he turned to look up at her, his eyes wide with surprise. It struck an unexpected familiarity with her.

He pulled one of the headphones off his ear and waved his hand to try to refuse the food.

"서비스†," she explained.

His eyes darted between her and the food several times before nodding, which she acknowledged with a smile before walking away to continue her cleaning. It was just a croissant, but she hoped it would take away a small bit of that sadness she saw in his eyes.

---

* 여기요 – yogiyo – here you go
† 서비스 – seobiseu – service (in Korean this term means the item is free or "on the house")

4

The bells at the front door jingled, making her think the croissant was a bad idea and it must have made the mystery man leave. Her disappointment was cut off by the sound of obnoxiously loud, slurred voices. A mix of octaves met her ears, and when she got a good look at them, she saw four men and two women stumbling into the café.

"Fuck," she whispered.

The drunks from the bars on the block, on several occasions, had confused her café with another bar where they could continue drinking. One of the young frat-looking guys stumbled to the counter, and she was assaulted by the smell of too much body spray, sweat, and alcohol.

"Can we get six shots of Cuervo?" he asked.

"Sir, this is a coffee shop, not a bar. Three doors down is the bar you want," she explained slowly, and even added some charades to give him directions.

"Six shots of Cuervo," he repeated slower, as if she were the one who didn't understand.

"Three doors down." She repeatedly pointed at the door for them to leave.

"Are you fucking stupid?" He got loud, leaning forward, bracing himself on the counter, crossing the threshold that was comfortable between employee and customer. "Six shots—"

"We are not a bar." She cut him off this time, not interested in trying to help anymore. "Please leave."

"Fuck this." The man tried to climb over the counter, his friends laughing and cheering him on, as Bridgette ducked to grab the pepper spray she kept below the cash register.

When she popped back up, he was no longer climbing over the counter but on the floor—with her singular patron's foot on his neck.

"This isn't a bar." The mystery man repeated her words slow and clear, as he pulled the mask covering his nose and lips away from his face.

"Holy shit," she whispered, knowing his face the second his

prominent nose with the freckle on the left side and thin lips were revealed. It was Woo Shin of CLAR1T.

"Now you and your friends get out," he ordered, his voice both soft and powerful.

The guy's friends were already halfway out the door before Woo Shin lifted his foot from the drunkard's neck. Finally, the terrified man scrambled to get up and wobbled to the door. As the bells settled, there was silence in the shop.

Bridgette was now alone with an idol from one of her favorite K-pop groups. Not just an idol, but her bias wrecker. The man who constantly made her question if Minhwa really was her favorite.

Woo Shin turned toward her, his worried eyes meeting hers. She didn't move. She couldn't. She was sure if she did, she would wake up from the most insane vivid dream ever. It was possible she could've fallen asleep. With all the late hours, maybe it was finally catching up to her. *Oh, what a vivid dream this is indeed.*

As the seconds passed, and no words were uttered as they stared at one another, his eyes went wide as he reached for his mask to try to cover his face again. But it was too late, she knew who he was and she was baffled as to how he had ended up at her café. Alone. At one in the morning.

"I should—" he started.

"You should—" she began simultaneously.

They laughed awkwardly, because what else could she do in such a bewildering situation? He motioned for her to speak first.

"You should probably get out of here. Those assholes might come back. It's happened before, and I wouldn't want you to get caught up in it if I have to call the cops," she explained.

"They're going to come back?" he asked.

"네. Well, possibly." She decided the best thing to do was start cleaning up again to get out of there before it could happen.

"Then I'm not leaving." He sat back down at the window, pulling the headphones from around his neck and packing them in his bag before keeping his eyes focused on the outside, like her own personal security guard.

"우 신 씨*..." She spoke his name and could see his body tense. His eyes met hers in the reflection of the window.

"너 내가 누군지 알아요†..." He pulled the mask off his face as he turned to face her and she once again took in his beauty.

"네." She bowed deeply. He may have been younger than her, but he was a respected public figure and she was just a café owner. "I didn't when you first walked in, if that makes you feel any better. It wasn't until you pulled down your mask that I realized it."

"Do you want a photograph? Autograph?" His tone was dejected. As if he were hoping no one would find him out.

And while she would've loved to have an autograph to hang on her wall in the shop, she chose to give him the space she could see he wanted.

"아니요‡. I would rather you get out of here just in case those idiots show up again. I'm sure your management wouldn't be thrilled if your name shows up on a police report while you're on your first American tour." She bowed before making her way back to the counter to finish cleaning. There was no response from him, but she also didn't hear the bells jingle to indicate he had left.

"가요§." She didn't bother to turn around as she began restocking the to-go cups and lids.

"안돼요#," he responded in a singsong tone. "If those guys come back—"

"I have pepper spray and an emergency button that goes directly to the cops. I'll be fine," she grumbled, meanwhile internally freaking out that he was so worried about her well-being and wanting to keep her safe.

She turned back around to face the front of the store when she realized he was no longer sitting at the table by the window but stood in her space behind the counter. She had to bend back in order to see his face.

---

* 우 신 씨 – u sin ssi – Woo Shin (formal)
† 너 내가 누군지 알아요 - neo naega nugunji al-ayo – You know who I am.
‡ 아니요 – aniyo – no
§ 가요 – gayo - go
# 안돼요 – andwaeyo - no

"What are you doing?" she asked nervously.

"If I help you finish all your tasks, would the owner allow you to leave early for the employee's safety?" He was rather elegant when he spoke English. She had read that Minhwa had been teaching them English for months leading up to the tour, since he was American, and from 우신's speaking, he was doing an amazing job.

"Being that I *am* the owner…" She trailed off to gauge his reaction. Which was equal parts surprised and impressed. She rolled her eyes to feign annoyance at his knight-in-shining-armor routine. "Fine. Help me finish packing up these pastries so I can donate them." She handed him gloves and the large brown bags she had been tossing the pastries into previously.

"That's very kind of you." His smile made his eyes nearly disappear, and those pearly whites of his were on full display. Her heart didn't know if it could handle being so close to that smile she had seen through the screen countless times.

She gave a quick nod before getting back to the restocking of the cups.

"You know my name," he said as he started to bag the pastries, "but I don't know yours."

"Does it matter?" she laughed as she moved on to the next task of cleaning out the coffee makers and dumping the used coffee beans into the trash bin.

"Does it not?" he questioned back.

"After you leave here, my name will leave as well." She turned her head to the side to see his eyes were solely focused on her. His hand frozen with a muffin about to be placed in a bag.

"Isn't that for me to decide?" He finally dropped the muffin into the bag.

He's smooth.

"Bridgette," she responded.

"예뻐*," he flirted. She caught the smirk on his lips, revealing one of the dimples on his cheeks. With it directed at her, she fully understood why her thoughts always swayed from her bias in music

---

* 예뻐 – yeppeo – pretty

videos, performances, and interviews. A smirk like that, directed at one person, could end up with that person becoming pregnant. Her ovaries were fighting with her to give him the chance to try.

"Who's your bias?" he asked. She abruptly stopped fumbling with the coffeepot.

"네?" she choked out, trying to play it cool. But it was impossible to ignore the fact that he had asked that question just as her brain was fighting itself over the same one.

"You knew who I was. You've mentioned the tour I'm on. I'm assuming you listen to our music. You know our group." He reached over to grab the coffeepot out of her hand and placed it on the counter.

"Yeah, I do know your music. My friend and I are CLARvoyants." She had no reason to hide it. Just like he would forget her name, he would forget her being a fangirl.

"And you still don't want a photo or autograph?" He raised an inquisitive brow as his eyes roamed her face. She took slow, deep breaths to hide the fact that her body was on fire with the heat emanating from his.

"I'm sure you're sick of people asking for those kinds of things in your free time. I can respect your time." She pointed up. "Plus, I can just save my security camera feed from tonight for posterity."

Their laughs commingled and she enjoyed their melody. As their laughter died down, he took a step toward the display case to finish packing up the pastries, and she went back to cleaning the coffeepots in silence.

"Now what?" he said, and she turned to see he had bagged up all the pastries and was standing, pulling off the gloves.

"I sweep and mop and then I'm done for the night. Brush the crumbs off yourself so we can get them all." She wiped her wet hands on her apron as she watched him miss several crumbs on his clothing. Once her hands were dry, she began swiping at the crumbs on his shirt to help get them all off.

He grabbed her wrist and pulled her hand away from him. Why was he stopping her? All she was trying to do was help him—

9

How stupid could I be? Touching an idol like he's my everyday employee, decrumbing each other's clothes!!

She bowed deeply and repeatedly, apologizing, "미안해요*. I shouldn't have touched you like that. Please forgive me. It's just that—"

On her last bow, he tugged her toward him, her body bumping into him as his other arm circled her waist to hold her close. That warmth she had felt from his body now made hers ignite.

"If you were to brush any lower, I wouldn't have been able to keep my composure," he whispered, his breath fanning across her face, a mix of his 아아 and the butteriness of the croissant she had served him.

"네?" she fumbled, trying to get him to release her wrist.

"While the look of those pastries," he nodded to the bags on the counter, "and the smell of coffee got me to glance through the window, you're the reason I walked in." The way his gaze darkened as he stared down at her put her whole body on high alert.

"Y-yo-you—" she stumbled, unable to process what he was saying as his arm around her waist squeezed, pressing her harder against his body.

And that's when she felt the hard truth of his "composure" statement against her stomach.

"Are you going to tell me?" His voice had gotten lower, his breath creeping over every inch of her exposed skin.

"Tell you what?" she whispered. Any louder and she wasn't sure actual words would've come out.

"Your bias," he answered, his head dipping down toward hers.

"Minhwa," she blurted out as she closed her eyes, unsure how she would react to what she thought was going to happen next. But nothing did. After what felt like ages, his arm unwrapped from her waist, and his hand dropped her wrist. She shivered from the cold; her body had become ice as the heat of his disappeared.

"아…미안해요," he whispered, causing her eyes to shoot open and see the disappointment on his face.

---

* 미안해요 – mianhaeyo – I'm sorry

10

"우 신—" she reached out to grab him but pulled back, knowing it would make things more awkward.

"So sweeping and mopping next?" Woo Shin finished brushing the rest of the crumbs off himself. He grabbed the broom from the corner and walked out from behind the counter to sweep the front, which made guilt bubble in her stomach.

"Please stop." She walked out and tried to grab the broom from him.

"Let's not make this any more awkward than I've already made it." He turned away from her, continuing to sweep.

In actuality Bridgette was the one who had made their whole situation awkward. If they completed the tasks quickly, the faster she could close up, the sooner he would leave. Then she could wallow in the most embarrassing moment of her life.

She went to the back kitchen to fill the mop bucket in the slop sink, and when she came back out, she saw him flipping up the chairs onto the tables to clear the floor.

"Done this before?" she asked.

"When we were still trainees, I wanted to make some extra cash. Minhwa had actually taught us how to help keep our debt to the company down by getting paid elsewhere." He continued explaining as he swiped crumbs into a pile. "There was a café down the block from our dorm, and I would work there to help them close up and clean. After hours, so that no one could come in, which ensured no one from the company would see me."

"How did you have time to rest?" she asked, as she began to mop the areas he had finished sweeping.

"No time for rest." The sad laugh that left his mouth had her heart clench.

She halted her movements to watch him continue to sweep as if he didn't have a care in the world. "우 신, that's terrible. I'm so sorry."

"There's that saying, I'll have time to sleep when I'm dead. I knew what I had signed up for," he paused "to an extent."

"What? Didn't expect all the adoring fans so fast?" she joked, trying to lighten the mood but wishing she could comfort him.

"More like I didn't expect the anxiety and crippling depression." His calm demeanor as he said something so upsetting made her blood run cold. "And coming to see myself as the 'least liked member' probably doesn't help."

She had been a K-pop fan for years and had seen what could happen to idols who reached their limits mentally and physically. She dropped the mop and ran over to him, wrapping her arms around his waist from behind. Feeling his torso go rigid, she squeezed harder.

"I know this won't miraculously change anything, but let me say, you matter." She spoke into his back. She felt him scoff, and his self-doubt crushed her soul. Letting go of him, she moved in front of him and met his eyes, which had that same saddened questioning look she had noticed when he first sat down in her café.

"CALR1T wouldn't be what it is if it weren't for you." She poked his chest. "Not just your voice but you producing 90 percent of the tracks. Your sound, your lyrics are what makes CLAR1T, CLAR1T." She grabbed his arm, shaking gently as if to shake her words into his mindset and fight those negative concepts in his head.

But his face confused her. His mouth hung open and his eyes were wide.

"뭐? Did I say something wrong?" She took a step back, wondering why he was caught off guard by her statement.

"How did you know I produce our songs?" he asked.

"What do you mean?" She was puzzled. *That* was what he took from her little pep talk?

"No one knows. How do *you* know?" He took a step closer to her.

"How is it not common knowledge?" She backed away as she explained, "ㅜㅜ97. It's a play on your name and your birth year. But now that I'm thinking about it, it also looks like tears, and suddenly it makes even more sense." She searched his face, trying to get a read on him.

"We did that so people wouldn't know I was a producer." He grabbed her shoulders. "Do other people know?"

She shrugged, surprised by the panic in his voice. "I don't have many people to talk CLAR1T with. Just my best friend. And with the café I don't have a lot of time to befriend other CLARvoyants. I have maybe spoken to a handful on social media." His grip on her shoulders released slightly. "Not to mention being 'older' has always been seen as a negative, so not many people want to befriend me."

"Older?" He gave her a once-over as if that would tell him how much older than him she was.

"네. Being a thirty-four-year-old who enjoys the music of a twenty-seven-year-old is apparently the worst thing I could be in this world." She scoffed, which got a small smirk out of him.

"So, no one else knows?" he asked as his hands left her shoulders, leaving a small bit of his heat. She wished it would stay longer.

"Can't say I have asked the millions of fans you have, but I've never seen anyone mention it. I always just assumed everyone knew. Clearly that isn't the case." She caught his jaw clench and unclench. She was uncertain as to why his producing CLAR1T's music was such a panicky subject for him. He should be proud of what he was able to accomplish with their management's smaller budget.

She took a chance. "Why hide it? Why hide such talent? It's admirable how hard you worked to create CLAR1T's unique brand of music."

"Being the least liked mem—"

She cut him off by covering his mouth.

"I won't listen if you're going to be self-deprecating," she reprimanded.

He grabbed her hand from his mouth, pulling it away but keeping hold of it as he rubbed the back with his thumb. The heat she had missed on her shoulders had navigated down to the touch of his hand holding hers.

"I didn't want people to know." His shoulders drooped forward, minimizing his tall and broad frame.

"But why?" She put her free hand over the one that stroked hers.

He was about to answer when loud drunks walked past the front window, causing him to drop his head and pull down the brim of his cap.

"No one is coming in." She watched as the group continued down the road. "I locked the door before I started to mop."

"어*." He nodded, standing straight again, but he wasn't getting back to the topic.

She didn't have the right to probe so much into his life and decisions, and he had no reason to tell her his logic. He did what he did for the reasons only he knew. That should be the end of it. Was she dying to know? Yes. But she knew pressing him to give her the answer when he didn't want to would end with him shutting down and leaving.

While she knew he needed to leave because he might be seen, and possibly due to whatever he'd planned for the rest of his night, she desperately wanted him to stay. Maybe somehow she could make him see how special he really was.

"Let's finish up here so we can get you back to your hotel." She dropped her hand from his to finish mopping.

"아니†!" he exclaimed. She jumped in surprise at how loud he was. His cheeks went red, and he shoved his hands in his pockets. "미안해요. I just…"

He trailed off, his mouth opening and closing wondering what he was struggling to say.

"Okay, well, let's finish this so you can go on with your night." She grabbed the mop to make quick work of the floor.

---

* 어 – eo - yes
† 아니 – ani - no

CHAPTER TWO

신 had no plans for the night—he'd just needed to get out of the hotel. With every event and show, he'd started to feel more suffocated by the managers, his lack of motivation and inspiration to produce new music, and the pressure to create another successful album. The world felt like it was closing in around him, and he needed something, anything, to keep his dark thoughts at bay.

His initial idea was to drown his anxiety and depression in alcohol. It was not a productive or necessarily safe way, but he wanted a quick fix for the night. After searching for the best low-key bars in the city, he'd arrived on the street and was struck by the scent of delicious brewing coffee instead of smoke and booze.

He followed the scent and arrived at a small café with large old-style windows adorned with flowerpots, filled with colorful flowers but also herbs that mixed with the scent of the coffee, making his mouth water. He peeked through the window and was struck by the strawberry-blonde woman behind the counter. Her smile as she stared at something on her phone had him involuntarily smiling with her. And when she started bopping her head and shaking her hips as she began to bag pastries, he chuckled at her carefree nature.

A heat in 우신's heart he thought had frozen years ago had suddenly reignited.

When she caught him staring, he decided instead of running away, embarrassed he had been seen, he would see if he could get what he needed from her carefree aura instead of the use of alcohol. When he walked in, the place offered comfort and relaxation with its big soft-looking couches, coffee tables covered in magazines, and more, smaller pots of flowers and herbs. Bookcases filled one wall from the front windows to the back wall, where she was working behind the counter. The intimate tables at the front windows, where only one or two people could sit, settled him.

It was a place to be alone, but with other people who also wanted to be alone. It was the perfect shop for him to take a breath and try to regain some kind of inspiration. Or at least make a game plan for how he could miraculously find inspiration.

After he had heard her respond to him in Korean, he knew he had found the right place. While surprised, it brought him comfort in this new environment. But when those drunk assholes showed up, his comfort was gone, and his protective instinct kicked into overdrive. The guy trying to jump the counter spurred 우신 to pounce into action, adrenaline coursing through his veins as he pulled the guy away from the counter, shoving him to the floor and putting his foot on the aggressor's neck.

After the group scurried off, his adrenaline rush fueled what he had been hoping to find that night. But it was cut short by Bridgette seeing his face. He could tell she recognized him.

She didn't freak out or panic; instead, she tried to get him to leave to save his privacy. And all he wanted to do was to continue protecting her.

They had finished cleaning the café, and his mind was still reeling from the fact that she knew he was the one producing CLAR1T's music. Not one fan during their countless fan meetings, hi-touches, or busking sessions had brought it up. He thought their secret had been kept.

When 우신 was only a trainee and their social media team began to post about all the members who would be debuting, he could see he wasn't getting the same kind of fanfare as the rest of the members. He became obsessed with checking the numbers and would read through the comments. There were so many positive ones for all the other members, and while there were some negative sprinkled in, he was receiving the most hate. No one in the company said anything, but he worried that since he wasn't as popular as the rest of the guys, the company would kick him out of the group.

And as those thoughts sank in, he worried that if fans found out he was the one who had created their music, it would cause them to be less successful. He had asked the company whether he would be able to stay in the group if he remained anonymous in the producing credits. They were confused by his request and tried to convince him that he should share the fact that he was the producer, but he wasn't convinced and begged them to keep him anonymous. They agreed and he debuted with CLAR1T to fans loving the music he created, in secret. And that had been enough.

The company was so impressed with his producing prowess, they pressured him to create the group's next album so it could be an even bigger success.

"You've got all your stuff?" she shouted from the back room, rattling him out of his thoughts. She shut off the lights in the front of the shop, only an exit light and the streetlamps now illuminating the café. She came out of the back room and approached him with a bag on her shoulder while holding the bags of pastries he had packed. He nodded as he waved the only thing he had brought with him—his cell phone.

They walked out of the café into the crisp late-night air, and she locked the door behind them before turning back toward him with that smile that had drawn him into the café in the first place. He noticed that with the lights off in the café, the glass created a two-way mirror effect, so he could no longer see inside.

"It was nice to meet you, 우 신. I'm a huge fan of yours, and with all the help you gave me tonight, I am an even bigger fan." Bridgette giggled and her cheeks flushed. She bit her alluring bottom lip as she glanced up at him.

He could tell she was trying to say goodbye, but he wasn't ready to leave her yet. What if those assholes came back? What if they were waiting for her in dark corners?

"Do you need help dropping off those bags?" He pointed to the ones she clutched in her hands.

"Don't you have to get back to your hotel? Won't your group-mates and management be worried where you are?" Though he knew she was saying what she thought he wanted to hear, he could see something in her eyes. Those sapphire blue eyes watched him with a hopeful gaze.

And in his gut, he felt she didn't want him to leave either.

"아니. I'm free from any group activities for the rest of the night." He leaned forward to grab one of the handfuls of bags from her hand.

The boys had a food-related code word they used whenever they wanted to escape for the night. One would text they were going to get something to eat, another would ask what they were eating, and that's when they would drop the code word. Once the food was named, all the members knew to cover for the one who was enjoying some freedom.

So far on their tour, 지훈* and 성준† had used their code phrases, and 우신 had to admit he was jealous they were enjoying their time in the US so much. He used his code phrase to get away from everyone, unlike the other two members who had found a partner for the night. He could consider Bridgette a partner, just not in the same sense.

"And you're choosing to run errands with a fangirl in your free time?" she laughed out her rhetorical question.

"네," he said simply, grabbing the bags in her other hand while he surveyed the area. "Which way are we going?"

Her mouth hung open in surprise as she walked quickly down the street, accepting his help. As he jogged to catch up with her, he admired how her swaying hair looked like golden waves in the light of the streetlamps.

---

* 지훈 – ji hun – Ji-Hun
† 성준 – seongjun - Seongjun

"부드러워*," he mumbled to himself, thankful the bags in his hands prevented him from reaching out to see just how soft her hair was.

"What?" She turned her gaze toward him.

"아니야†, 아니야." He shook his head to get those thoughts out of his mind. If she had heard him, there would have been another embarrassing encounter like back in the café. She had made it clear which group member she liked, and it wasn't him, which wasn't surprising.

So why was he following her like a lost puppy? *Shouldn't I just quit while I'm already behind?*

He made the decision that once he helped her drop off the pastries, he would make a quick exit and leave her be. He still had the rest of the night to find some kind of inspiration for CLAR1T's next album, and he couldn't waste time on his personal desires.

They walked several blocks and he took in the sights and smells of a new city. The streets felt alive, even at that late hour. It reminded him of Seoul. He was bound to find what he desperately needed in this lively city.

They arrived at a four-story brick townhome and she climbed up the stairs ahead of him, which was a small form of torture as her hips swayed her nicely rounded behind in his face.

She rang the intercom bell; a loud buzz sounded, and she pulled the door open. Holding the door for him to enter first, she then led him down a small brightly lit hallway. Unique lighting fixtures in the shapes of animals hung above bulletin boards filled with informative pamphlets, names, pictures, and children's art. A large calendar contained lists of chores and other responsibilities for what he assumed were the long-term residents of the shelter.

"This is a homeless shelter?" he asked.

"아니요." She shook her head. "A women's shelter. If you see any kids running around, let me know."

---

* 부드러워 – budeuleowo – soft

† 아니야 – aniya - nothing

"여기*? At this hour?" He spun around to see if anyone was nearby.

"It's sometimes the only time moms can see their kids. They tend to get the jobs with late or odd hours, either because they go to school during the day, or they get better pay for the night shifts. The kids defy their bedtimes to spend time with their moms." She pushed open a swinging door that led into a large industrial kitchen. "Speaking of…"

The sound of something closing drew his attention to the back of the kitchen. There stood a young boy, wide-eyed and mouth outlined in what looked to be melted ice cream.

"Bridgette!" the young boy shouted as he trotted over to her.

"*Shhh.*" She brought a finger to her mouth with a little smile that made the young boy smile as well. "Cam, you know the rules. You should be in bed right now. I can't keep covering for you, ya know."

"I was waiting for you so I could get my mom your chocolate waffle before they're all gone at breakfast." He smiled, and when he turned to see 우신, he noticed that one of the boy's front teeth was missing. "I know him."

Bridgette turned to 우신 with a nervous smile and somewhat frantic eyes. "Oh he's just—"

"I'm 우신. Your name is Cam?" He crouched down to eye level, taking in the chocolate brown of the young boy's eyes.

"Yeah…wait…우신?" Cam's eyes darted from Bridgette to 우신 several times before going wide. "Bridgette, don't you like a guy in one of your bands with that name?" His eyes continued to dart between the two of them. "Yes! The group you were supposed to see in concert tonight. You got to go and were able to bring them to the house to help? That's so cool!"

"I sadly couldn't go. Amanda got sick, so I had to cover for her," she explained as she took the bags from 우신 and plopped them on the metal countertop in the middle of the kitchen. Then she started grabbing serving dishes from above the counter.

---

* 여기 – yeogi -here

"But you still get to hang out with your…" Cam trailed off, his face scrunching as he was thinking. "What do you call it again?"

There was a long pause as 우 신's eyes went to Bridgette's, his heart hammering with hope.

"Wrecker. Bias wrecker."

CHAPTER THREE

Bridgette said it. Out loud. In front of the bias wrecker himself. The whole night she had been trying to be calm, cool, nonchalant, and keep a distance to avoid any sort of delusion that him spending time helping her was anything more than trying to maintain his kind and caring image. But now 우 신 was very aware of her fanaticism.

"Bias wrecker?" He craned his neck as he turned his head to look up at her, a smug smirk on his thin lips, the tips of his ears, poking out from his hat, reddening.

"You only asked for my bias." She continued trying to keep her collected persona, as internally her stomach had dropped to her butt. Turning away from both, she pulled out two chocolate waffles from one bag and wrapped them in a large napkin.

"Here, Cam. Now go back to you and your mom's room and go to sleep. I know you have school in the morning," she reprimanded.

Cam grabbed the napkin with his large gap-toothed grin and a thank you before walking back over to 우 신, who had stood from his crouching position.

"Thanks for making Bridgette happy again." Cam wrapped his

arms around 우 신's legs before running out of the kitchen, his loud footsteps pounding up the stairs.

The kitchen became silent. He was watching her and she wasn't about to explain what Cam meant unless she absolutely had to. She began unpacking pastries onto the large serving trays as he came to her side and followed suit.

"What did Cam mean?" 우 신 was the one to break the silence, and she cringed at how quickly she had to explain. She'd hoped she would have more time to compose her thoughts. "About me making you happy again?"

"Kids, ya know?" She tried to laugh off the incident. *Think, Bridgette! Think!*

"You can tell me, Bridgette." He grabbed her hand before it went back into one of the bags. "Like you've said a couple times tonight, I will forget once I leave here."

"I'm sure it's nothing you haven't heard before." She rolled her eyes, removing her hand from his to finish plating the bag of waffles. "I was struggling with self-doubt and my decision to open my café a few months ago. I was so sure it and I were going to be huge failures before I opened the doors on the first day. I found your music by accident when it played on a station I had on at the shop while I was doing some final taste tests on new products I was going to launch to attract more customers. At first, I obviously didn't know what you all were saying, but something about it stuck with me."

As she finished plating and grabbed the plastic wrap to cover the plate, she continued with the story. "I decided to search online for translations and as I read through the lyrics, some of the songs really hit home. I related to thinking so little of myself. The feeling of giving up before I even started. And not realizing that there were people who loved me for who I was and what I've done. And the fact that I wouldn't have some of those people in my life if I didn't do something as big and scary as opening up my own place. I realized it would be okay if I did fail because of everything I learned and the friends I've made."

There was silence beside her. She wasn't sure why she expected him to come back with a quick remark, but when she peered over at him, she saw his eyes were glossy and his jaw was clenching and unclenching.

"우 신?" She moved closer to make sure he was okay, and in less than a second, his arms were wrapped around her waist, pulling her up against him, causing her to lift onto her tiptoes as his face buried in her neck. The brim of his cap pushed into her collarbone, which made her try to back up, but instead he grabbed it and ripped it off his head, slamming it on the counter beside them. It was the first time she could see his whole head. And more specifically, the hair she always told Sophia was his best look.

But that moment wasn't the time to fangirl about his hair. She felt his chest rise and fall unsteadily, his warm breath choppy against her collarbone, and she knew. She knew he needed to let out that silent cry. It had been brewing for a while. She noticed it in the shop when he first walked in.

She wrapped her arms around him and began rubbing his back, cooing, "괜찮아*."

After a few minutes, his breaths steadied and he whispered into her shoulder, "고마워†."

"Why are you thanking me? I should be thanking you." She gently pushed him away so she could get a good look at him. But he turned his head away, attempting to hide his red puffy eyes and tear-stained cheeks. He tossed his hat back onto his head, covering up his gorgeous hair once again and hiding his face in the shadow of the brim. It didn't hide very much, however. His nose was slightly runny, so she grabbed a napkin to let him blow his nose as she used her thumbs to brush away the tears on his cheeks.

"No one." He choked out, "No one has ever said anything like that to me."

"No fucking way," she responded incredulously. He shook his head. "Well, now someone has, and now you know the power of the music you produce."

His lips began to quiver when she said that, and she instinctively

---

* 괜찮아 - gwaenchanh-a – it's okay
† 고마워 – gomawo – thank you

traced her thumb over them to calm him down. Thinking of every-thing he had opened up to her about, she wondered if he had anyone to talk to back in Korea or on tour. But she knew the answer to that question from what she had seen that night. Maybe he had walked into her café for his own reasons, but maybe fate decided to intervene so she could help him. She couldn't save him, but maybe she could convince him to see someone who could help.

"You work so hard, 우 신, you should allow yourself to be praised for all your dedication to CLAR1T. I'm not sure where you got this idea that you're not as talented or as popular as the rest of your group." She saw his lips about to open to argue, so she pressed her thumb to stop him. "You are all talented in your own way. And your music and lyrics are what bring everyone else's talents to life. You're the glue."

He tried to speak again, but she pressed her thumb harder. "That's a lot of pressure. And that's why you were by yourself in my shop. You needed space to breathe, right? So the world didn't feel like it was crashing in around you?"

Bridgette was speaking from experience. She didn't have the same level of pressure as millions of adoring fans and a music label could create, but she felt pressure from family and friends about her business and its success. The struggle to come up with new unique types of pastries and drinks to attract people and keep them coming back. That's why she related to his creations, his lyrics, and his music.

His shoulders relaxed and his head drooped. She wrapped her arms around his waist to give him another hug. She had nestled into his chest now that he was standing straighter.

"알아*, 알아, 알아," she cooed.

One of his hands gripped her cheek to get her to look up at him. His dark eyes met hers before she watched them trail down her face and stop at her lips.

If he does try to kiss me again, I'm letting it happen.

His eyes left her lips, his hand dropped from her cheek, and that

---

* 알아 – al-a – I know

bothered her. She knew he had done it because of what happened in the café, and that was understandable. So she made the move instead. She grabbed both sides of his face and pulled his gaze back to her as she lifted onto her tiptoes to press her lips against his.

She worried he would push her away, thinking she was kissing him out of pity or sympathy, but instead he reacted instantly by putting his hands back on her waist and pulling her closer to him. His lips parted and devoured hers. She would never be able to drink her café's coffee without thoughts of him and his taste. It would be a memory etched in her mind and heart for the rest of her life. It was intoxicating, and she was desperate for more.

She lowered her hands to his chest, where she could feel his heart racing at an equal speed to her own.

He squeezed her waist, causing her to jump, which must've been what he wanted, because her feet were no longer on the ground as he maneuvered her quickly. The backs of her legs felt the edge of the table where they had been plating pastries only moments before. She could feel the chill of the metal on her butt as fire coursed through the rest of her body.

A nudge of his hip on her knee and she spread her legs to allow him to fit in between. It was like their bodies could read one another. Each knew what the other wanted without having to ask. One of his hands on her waist dipped under her blouse, and his fingers on her skin caused her to moan into his mouth as that fire within her erupted into a blaze that couldn't be put out. His tongue dove onto her mouth to cover the moan and play with her tongue as he groaned, pulling her closer to the table's end, his groin pressing against her center.

"Bridgette," his voice rasped out between their kisses.

"우 신," she responded, as her lips moved to his jawline and down his neck.

"Maybe we should—"His words cut off as she nipped as his collarbone. "씨발*," he moaned, giving her all the confirmation she needed to keep going. Her hands scratched down his clothed torso

---

* 씨발 – ssibal - fuck

27

to the edge of his shirt and pushed past it. She felt his heated skin, his abdomen tightening at her touch, and she started moving her hands upward.

That was until a throat cleared to their side, and his lips left hers to turn away so the intruder couldn't catch a glimpse of him. Bridgette turned her head toward the person to see Marly, the night shift "mom" as they called her, leaning on the doorframe holding the door open with the goofiest grin on her face.

"Didn't mean to interrupt." She laughed as Bridgette removed her hands from 우신's torso and tried to shimmy off the table. But he wasn't moving. Instead, she felt his lips press to her shoulder.

Is he crazy?! Marly is right here!

In her frantic panic, she gently pushed him, which made him finally move away so she could get down from the counter.

"I heard some noises in the hall, caught Cam running up to his room and he said you had arrived with the pastries. Didn't mention you had company." Marly gave 우신 a once-over.

"Oh…uh…yeah." Bridgette tried to cover her lips, as if that would hide the fact that she had just been caught making out with him. "Marly, this is 우신. 우신, Marly."

Bridgette awkwardly introduced the two, and 우신 bowed while Marly stared at him as a massive smile grew on her face.

"우신?" Marly turned back to Bridgette. "*The* 우신?"

If Bridgette could've crawled deeper into the hide-from-total-humiliation hole, she would. But there was nowhere to go and nowhere to hide, and so she had to accept that he was going to learn just how much of a fangirl she was. She nodded in acknowledgement of that fact.

"How did you make *that* happen?" Marly joked as she patted Bridgette on the shoulder. "Good for you." Marly grabbed one of the trays of pastries they had been plating. "Let's get these in the fridge so y'all can enjoy the rest of your night." She winked and made her way to the large walk-in to put the pastries away.

우신 said nothing but had the goofiest grin on his face when he put his hat back on his head and grabbed a couple trays to help Marly, while Bridgette finished plating what was left.

Bridgette's mind was still processing what had just happened. What *she* had initiated. His lips, while thin, were tender and demanding. The feeling of his moan on her mouth when she kissed down his neck sent heat back down between her legs. She had to pinch herself multiple times to: A. make sure she wasn't dreaming, and B. stay focused on the task at hand.

And he not only kissed me back, he was trying to do more! So much for the pinching.

The closing of the fridge snapped her back to the reality that they had finished plating and putting away all the pastries.

"Well," Marly put her hand on Bridgette's shoulder and continued, "you're free now. Enjoy the rest of your night. 우 신, it was very nice to meet you. Hope we see you again."

"Nice meeting you as well." He bowed.

"Marly, if you could maybe not mention what you saw." Bridgette knew what could potentially happen to 우 신 if word got out that he was seen kissing someone. Not just a media circus, but he could be removed from the group and dropped from the company entirely.

"My lips are sealed." She made a motion of locking her lips before leaning over to Bridgette and whispering, "Unlike yours and his before I interrupted."

Bridgette turned bright red as Marly giggled and walked out of the kitchen, leaving the two of them alone once again.

It was awkward. But she didn't get the sense he felt the same way. His smile said something else entirely. He pulled off his hat for the second time that night, running his hand through the loose strands from his bun. He pushed it away from his cheek, only for it to return to shape his face, touching his cheekbones.

"I don't want to keep you from going home, Bridgette," he started. It confused her. Had she done something wrong? Was she that bad of a kisser that he was now desperate to get away from her? "If you can just point me in the direction of a low-key—"

"Do you want to get a drink?" She cut him off. She wanted to spend more time with him, even though she had previously tried to play aloof. Even after she had tried to get him to leave her café. He had helped her with the drunkards, found out about her being a fangirl, she kissed him, and he kissed her back. If he turned her down, she knew the night really was over for them.

He dropped his head, his hair that wasn't in the bun falling in front of his face a bit. She wanted to run her hands through it so badly, and it took everything in her to keep her hands by her sides. She tried to calm her breathing as she waited for his answer that could change the trajectory of her whole night and possibly her whole life. When he lifted his head again, a smirk on his face, his eyes filled with an electric charge that easily pulsed through her.

"좋아*," he responded.

He might not have meant for his movements to be seductive, but they made Bridgette shudder with desire.

"갈까?†" She nudged him toward the kitchen doors so they could hit their next destination.

AFTER A SHORT, SEXUALLY CHARGED BUT SILENT CAB RIDE, THEY arrived outside the bar. The surrounding street was dead silent, with all the other establishments closed for the night. But she knew that inside the one they stood in front of, other restaurateurs, bartenders, cooking and wait staff would be having a few drinks and unwinding after a long night.

"Are you sure this place is open?" He surveyed the area. Taking in how truly silent the city street was.

She laughed at his obvious concern as she knocked on the door. It swung open and the tall, broad, bald-headed, fully-tatted bouncer stepped out. The wrinkle between his eyebrows that was in its permanent scrunch of scrutiny, and his deep frown upon seeing Bridgette, changed in an instant. His eyes lit up like a child's and his smile was filled with delight.

"Bridgey!" He wrapped her in his death grip of a bear hug,

---

* 좋아 - joh-a – sounds good
† 갈까? - galkkayo? – shall we go?

lifting her off the ground shortly before placing her back onto the concrete.

"Hey, Hank!" She chuckled as she softly punched his hard-as-a-rock bicep. While she was play fighting him, she watched his eyes land on her guest, and his demeanor changed.

"Who's this guy?" He reverted back to his towering brick-wall stance as his eyes stayed on 우 신 and his eyebrows scrunched back to assessment mode.

"He's a new friend of mine. He's only in town tonight, so I thought I would show him our little world," she explained to calm Hank's territorial nature toward newbies.

Hank puffed out his chest as he took a step closer to 우 신, giving the once-over with a huff. 우 신 didn't back down, which was impressive as most people tended to cower when Hank invaded their space the first time meeting him. 우 신 looked more confused than anything, making Bridgette laugh at their interaction.

"Stop trying to scare him, Hank." Bridgette grabbed 우 신's hand and pulled them around Hank's frame and through the door, into the bar.

Several patrons turned to the bar entrance and, upon seeing her, gave a small greeting as she pulled 우 신 toward the bar. She shouted her hellos and pointed to 우 신, introducing him as simply a friend from the café. When they finally got to the bar and sat on barstools, she let out an exhausted huff.

"You're popular," he said with a warm smile.

She laughed. "We all help each other. We're like a big family. Like you and your CLAR1T team."

She watched his warm smile fade, the small gleam in his eyes diminishing little by little until it was gone completely.

"Are you and the other members not close?" she probed. She knew they weren't friends who just formed a band because they liked music. That wasn't how the world of K-pop worked. They were manufactured. Put together because their jointness was sellable.

She felt that she had asked a very personal question maybe she shouldn't have. But they had opened up about a few things throughout the night, which made her believe they had built a small level of trust. It made her feel comfortable asking. Maybe it was a step too far into the personal.

"They're not the problem. They're what keeps me sane, if I'm being honest." His appreciation for the boys was evident when he boasted, "It's more the other aspects of CLAR1T. The rest of the team. The production team. Our company's pressure for me to make our next album bigger and better than our debut." She realized he had never let go of her hand and was squeezing it hard.

She squeezed back, letting him know she was there for him, and words weren't necessary.

"Who's the new guy?" a voice from behind the bar interrupted.

"Stephanie, this is 우 신. 우 신, Stephanie." She once again introduced him to someone who was all too familiar with his name. When there was a lull in response, Bridgette knew what was about to come out of Steph's mouth.

"*The* 우 신?" Stephanie responded in the same way Marly had.

"Maybe I need to change my name to *The* 우 신." He chuckled, bowing his head to Stephanie and then turning his focus back toward Bridgette. "You mention me a lot for not being your bias."

"He isn't your favorite?" Steph sounded shocked, meanwhile Bridgette was thankful the bar was dark and he couldn't see just how red she was turning.

"Can we get two pints of whatever is on tap tonight?" Bridgette chose to ignore both of their little playful teases and placed her order.

"Yeah, yeah." Steph rolled her eyes and grabbed two large glasses, then tilted them under the tap to pour the golden-yellow brew.

"You talk about us a lot, it seems." He smirked the cockiest smirk. His hand, which had been squeezing hers out of nervousness, now loosened, and his thumb caressed the top of her hand gently.

"You're my ult group, so I guess it makes sense." While she was trying desperately to play it cool around him, the fact that so many people had outed her was most likely enough to have him questioning why he chose to continue spending time with her.

Actually, why was he still sitting next to her? Why didn't he run away after the third person mentioned her fascination with him? Why did he let her kiss him after finding out what a big fan she was? And why did he kiss her back?

She opened her mouth to ask, but the two beers clanked down on the bar counter, startling her.

"I'll pay for these." Releasing her hand, he pulled his bag onto his lap to grab his wallet.

"No money here." Stephanie waved off the cash and walked away to serve another patron.

"How do they make money?" he leaned over and whispered in Bridgette's ear, sending warm tingles down her spine.

"During normal operating hours." She took a large swig from her beer. "Now they only serve what's opened. Once the bottle is gone, that booze is gone and it's done. We all come here after our shifts. It's only open for two hours to unwind and release the stress of the day and night with likeminded people. Everything that happens or is said in here, stays in here."

"We do something similar." He grabbed his beer, clanking it against hers before bringing it to his lips, his eyes solely focused on her, keeping those tingles coursing to every nerve ending. Had it gotten ten degrees hotter in the bar?

"You do?" she asked softly, as she caught his eyes moving to her lips while she spoke.

"네. After a show we get pretty high on adrenaline. To the point that we can't sleep. We usually go out into whatever city we're in until the early morning hours, and while we're enjoying the food and drinks, the city around us gets quiet, and it relaxes us. It is a small sense of freedom." His shoulders dropped as if some of the weight she had noticed earlier left his body. "But sometimes we want real freedom. Those nights, like tonight, we individually search for our own ways to relax or find a different kind of adrenaline rush."

"And your way of relaxing is helping an old fangirl by kicking out annoying drunks from her café, donating pastries, and listening to her supposed friends tell you how *big* of an old fangirl she is?" Bridgette laughed as she brought her beer back to her lips.

"당연하지*!" he joked, and the bright smile that ran across his face as he laughed clenched her heart. She hadn't seen a smile that bright from him in months. During the fansigns, concerts—any recent photos or videos really—she always felt his smile was forced. She chalked it up to her mind tricking her into reading way too much into it and her being a weird fangirl. But after some of the things he had said, and things she had seen that night, her intuition hadn't been off.

"누나†, I'm enjoying myself. Don't overthink it." His hand reached out to swipe some of the beer's foam off her upper lip as he spoke. Her eyes went wide, and those tingles became full-blown electrical currents that could power an entire city block.

누나. He just called her 누나. Her mind had stopped all proper functioning after hearing him speak such a simple word. 누나... It was playing on repeat in her head. She had wondered what it would sound like to be called 누나. And it was more erotic than she could've ever imagined.

"괜찮아?‡" His hand moved from her upper lip to cupping her cheek.

"Are you playing at something?" She glanced around the bar. "Is this some kind of hidden camera sho—"

He kissed her, cutting off her words. She pinched her thigh, hard, to confirm once again she wasn't dreaming. She reached out to grab his shirt, pulling him closer, drawing him off his barstool, his backpack falling to the ground. He had towered over her but now bent down so that his lips never left hers.

His other arm circled her waist, forcing her body closer, pressing up against one another. The room around them melted away. Nothing except for the two of them existed. That was until...

"Get a room, you two!" Stephanie shouted, and suddenly the cheers and clapping reminded Bridgette they weren't alone, and the

---

* 당연하지 - dang-yeonhaji – of course
† 누나 – nuna – older sister for male (can be used as a term of flirtation or closeness between a younger guy and older woman.)
‡ 괜찮아? - gwaenchanh-a? – are you ok?

room hadn't actually disappeared. She tried to pull her lips away, but he wasn't letting up as easily, and his tongue swiped at her bottom lip before she tapped his chest to get him to stop.

He slowly pulled his lips from hers and rotated his head to bow in apology to Stephanie. He turned back to Bridgette, licking his lips as he stared down at hers.

She covered them in shock. "You kissed——"

"You kissed me first in the kitchen." He took her hand to unblock her mouth, his eyes refocused on her lips.

"You called me 누나," she blurted.

He leaned back as a loud laugh filled her ears, even catching the attention of more of the other patrons in the bar.

"If I knew this would be the reaction, I would've called you 누나 sooner." His arm around her waist gave a squeeze, pressing her closer to him, and she felt what she had felt in the café, but much more aroused, pressing firmly against her stomach.

She did a double take between them to see if she was right.

"I've never done anything like this before but…" He trailed off, bringing her focus back to him. His deep night sky-like eyes perusing her face. "About that room she mentioned…"

"Already called you guys a car when you first started making out," Steph interrupted once again.

"Jesus, Steph." Bridgette jumped but couldn't move much as his hand was still strongly holding her waist.

"You would've turned him down for some stupid reason. I stopped you from doing that." Steph grabbed her phone. "Oh look, it's outside. Enjoy!"

Bridgette set her eyes back to 우신. His stare was focused on her as he nudged his head in the direction of the exit. His stare sent a lustful gaze down at her, igniting that fire between her legs once more and sending shocks of electricity through her body.

"Are you sure?" she whispered nervously.

He tugged her waist harder against him, the corner of his lips curling into a smirk, his darkened gaze holding hers.

"Since I stepped foot in your café, I have been sure." His voice dropped to a near growl, which continued that electricity launching through her body. "누나."

He was teasing her. But with that joyful smile, those sultry eyes, and that singular word, she didn't need any more convincing. She grabbed his hand on her waist, spun out of his hold, jumped off the stool, snatched his backpack off the floor, and made their way back out of the bar.

"And don't worry, we don't know who he is and we never saw you two here," Stephanie shouted, and several patrons yipped in agreement.

Outside of the bar sat a large, black SUV with colorful under-glow lighting up the street below it and loud music thumping that caused her body to vibrate. It had to be their ride.

I'm really bringing 우 신 *back to my apartment to do…* Her mind couldn't finish the sentence. The prospect of what she was about to do with someone she had never in a million years thought she would interact with was swirling around her mind.

He moved around her and pulled open the back door of the car to allow her entrance, the music filling the empty street. His face held an expression she wished to see more of in the future, on stage and off: excitement.

With that vision, she climbed into the car. *I'm bringing* 우 신 *back to my place.*

CHAPTER FOUR

신 hadn't felt the rush of stepping into the unknown in years. But being around Bridgette had inspired him in the short span of a few hours, and he needed more of it in his life. He had been so focused on success and the pressure to complete the album that his life fell to the wayside. Now his mind felt like it had flipped a switch and had finally shut up about what was expected of him; his anxiety was not only being held at bay, but it was nowhere to be found in that moment It was exhilarating. He almost felt like the young boy with the dream of making it big, motivated by that passion again.

When they had climbed into the SUV, he instinctively went all the way to the back bench instead of the two center seats. That was always his safe space in the company vans and SUVs. Less light made it easy for him to hide so his managers couldn't pressure him on the rides to each event CLAR1T would be promoting at or performing for. Bridgette didn't question his motives and moved from her original seat in the middle to the back.

He wanted her. He never denied it and he made it clear several times that night. But after having his small tastes of her, he knew it wouldn't be enough to curb the hunger. Her lips were soft against his, and when they pressed for more, he wanted to give her everything he had to offer. Her hands against his body warmed his soul. She made him feel alive. A feeling he, again, hadn't felt in several years. Not to mention her words from the café stuck with him. They played on repeat in his head. Two simple words and he felt bare in front of her. A total stranger.

You matter.

He turned to look at Bridgette, who'd turned her face to the window, watching the skyline as the SUV drove down the road. He could only make out her profile when the car passed streetlights or car headlights coming from the other direction, but he caught her teeth picking at her bottom lip. An anxious tic he knew all too well.

The driver's music blasted through the car, vibrating the seats and windows. But when the latest song ended, 우신 could still feel light thumping on the seat. He found the culprit to be Bridgette's finger-tapping—another sign of her nervousness. Smiling, he placed his hand over hers, and her head snapped in his direction. He didn't want her to feel uncomfortable with him. If she was unsure of what they had proposed to one another, he would back off.

As the lights from outside the car once again gave him quick snippets of her face, he saw a soft smile as she stared at their connected hands. His hope of being with her was restored.

"미인이네*," he whispered as the next song started to play. Her face scrunched and she leaned closer to hear him. He repeated the phrase, but she shook her head, not understanding. "You're beautiful. You know that, right?"

He cupped her cheek, his thumb tracing her pouted bottom lip gently. It was still a bit swollen from their kiss in the bar, which only made him want to kiss her more. Her cheeks flushed and he could feel the heat on his hand. Leaning over, he closed the distance between them, and his nose grazed hers. He wanted to kiss her so badly, but he thought she would be worried about making a scene. She had stopped every other kiss between them when someone had walked in or said something. He would've happily continued to kiss

---

* 미인이네 - miin-ine – you're a beauty

her and probably more if she didn't push him away. He wasn't about to make her feel uncomfortable, so he decided to move away. He could wait until they arrived wherever it was.

He began to pull back but before he got far, her hand grabbed the back of his head and her lips pressed against his. All semblance of decorum was gone the second he got another taste of her lips. He slid closer to her, making her lean against the back of the seat. His hands moved to her hips and slipped under her shirt to feel her heated soft skin. Her stomach tensed slightly, and he was about to remove his hands when she let out a soft giggle against his lips.

"누나는 간지럼을 잘 타네?"* He leaned farther up against her to gently whisper against the shell of her ear as his fingers continued to glide up and down her stomach. When he pulled back to hear what she had to say, he saw her biting her lip, her eyes closed, and her head tipped all the way back, almost against the window. He still could only see her in the bursts of light, but he caught a sexy smirk, and he knew she was biting her lip to hold back her moans, her body arching up to meet his.

It only tempted him to get more of a reaction from her, so his hands moved down to the button of her jeans. As her eyes shot open, her hand that had been gripping the seat cushion reached down to stop him.

"우 신 미쳤냐?" † She hissed as her head turned toward the front of the car. 우 신 looked too to find the driver was tapping the steering wheel to the beat of the song pulsing in the car. The man was paying zero attention to what was happening in the back seat of his car.

"어, 미쳤어‡," he agreed smugly as he brought his fingers to her chin, pulling her gaze back to him. "He can't see us, and with how loud his music is, I doubt he can hear us...unless you're a screamer."

---

* 누나는 간지럼을 잘 타네? - nunaneun ganjileom-eul jal tane? – Are you ticklish noona?

† 우 신 미쳤냐? - u sin michyeossnya? – Woo Shin are you crazy?

‡ 어, 미쳤어 - eo, michyeoss-eo – yes I am crazy

He could feel her mouth open and close in shock as his fingers moved from her chin to her jaw and down her neck, following her gulps of air. His hand continued down to the valley of her chest, where he discovered her breathing had picked up, then on toward her stomach and back down to the button of her jeans. His stare never left hers.

"Just say no and I will stop." He pecked her lips.

"Don't stop," she responded as her hands moved toward his waistband.

"If at any point you *do* want me to stop, say the word," he whispered, his fingers pulling at her jeans and feeling the button pop open. He grabbed the zipper gently and dragged it down, giving him a tiny bit of access to what he wanted desperately.

His fingers tripped along the elastic band of Bridgette's panties before pressing his palm to her stomach and gently sliding his fingers down into the warmth between her legs. She arched up to meet his hand and her mouth hung open, calling him to cover it with his own.

When a finger slipped between her folds, he moaned as her pleasure coated his finger instantly. She was as aroused as he was, and that spurred him to slip a second finger in and find her clit to rub in soft circles. One of her hands gripped his waistband while the other went to the back of his head, her fingers grabbing his hair, pulling most of it from his hair tie.

He circled on and around her clit, then slid through her folds, her arousal dripping, giving him the encouragement he needed to thrust his fingers inside her. Her grip on his hair tightened as her other hand finally pushed into his pants, cupping his cock through his boxer briefs. He was hard as a fucking rock from the excitement of knowing that she was no longer worried about what the driver could or couldn't see, even though he knew they were cloaked in darkness that far back in the car. He could easily fuck her thoroughly back there and the driver wouldn't even notice. But she wasn't ready for that. And he still had to remain alert to whether people recognized him.

Her inhibitions had been flung out the window, and he was

determined to keep it that way. At least until he could make her cum on his fingers and see what else she was willing to try in the back seat of the car.

"You're so desperate for my fingers." He groaned as his fingers curled inside her, making her grind to get them deeper. "I can feel you pulsing around them."

"Tell me—" She choked on her words as he curved his fingers inside her again. Her hand squeezed his cock harder. Her eyes opened wide, totally focused on him. "Tell me what you want."

His cold heart, which he thought was dead, started thumping powerfully in his chest. It wasn't that lust-filled gaze in her eyes or the way she desperately moaned as his fingers moved inside her warmth. It was the fact that no one had ever felt the need to ask what *he* wanted. Whether it was in his popstar life or his personal one, no one seemed to care what he desired. But there, in the dark back seat of an SUV, a woman whom he had only known a few hours was begging for him to tell her.

He must've been in his own thoughts for too long because she moved her hand away from his cock and squirmed a bit under him, her hand reaching up to his cheek.

"왜-왜-왜 그래?*" she stuttered, panic in her tone.

"괜찮아,†" he cooed as he spread his fingers inside of her, making her gasp. Her hand left his cheek grabbing the collar of his shirt.

"Now to answer your question." His thumb began circling her clit and his fingers found the rhythm that made her walls clench. "I want to get you to cum at least twice in this car before we get to our destination."

That made her inner walls clench even harder around his fingers. "I enjoy feeling you tighten around me, 누나."

Her hand tugged on his hair as she pushed herself up to plant her lips on his. Her tongue traced his bottom lip and he gave her the entrance she desired. Her hips bucked to continue meeting his

---

* 왜 그래? - wae geulae? – What's the matter?

† It's okay

fingers, and his thumb kept circling her clit. She was so close to cumming that his own body pulsed with pleasure. He not only wanted to feel her around his cock, but he was desperate to taste her, and he wasn't sure which one he wanted to do first.

"누나," he whispered into her ear as his thumb pressed her clit, and he felt the first rush of an orgasm coat his fingers as her hand pulled at his hair and she brought her face into his chest to let out a rather loud moan.

She might actually be a screamer, he thought, excited to hear more from her.

"Fuck," was the first real word she said as she pulled her face away from his chest, her breathing still quick. Her hand dropped from his hair and she lay back, satiated. But he wasn't done with her yet. Like he said, he wanted her to cum at least twice during the car ride.

"How much farther until we're there?" he asked.

She turned her head toward the window, appearing to read the street signs as they passed.

"I think about five minutes." She turned back toward him.

"Not much time, but we can get it done." He smirked.

"Get wha—" Before she could finish the statement, he wrapped his free arm around her waist and lifted her off the back seat bench. He kept her chest against his, his fingers still nice and deep inside her, and moved her to straddle him.

"You asked what I want, and now I want you to ride these fingers just like you will my cock later," he said against her lips.

Her nervousness vanished into thin air. She had opened up to the fun of getting pleasure while there was a small possibility they could get caught. Her mouth hung open as her hips ground against his hand, his fingers happily curling to meet the spot inside her that made her pulsate around them.

"That's right, 누나. Just like that." His hand snaked around her waist and down to grab her ass, pressing himself up and pushing his fingers farther, which made her let out the loudest moan he had gotten from her so far.

"씨발." He groaned as his lips danced around her neck, trying to get another loud moan from her. Looking over her shoulder, his eyes met another pair of eyes. *Oops.* Unbothered by being caught, he turned his attention back to Bridgette.

She grabbed his now rather loose bun of hair and pulled his mouth away from her neck. She was about to speak when the car came to a halt, jerking them forward slightly. The sudden motion made his hand in her pants press against her clit and she dropped her head to his shoulder, her teeth biting his skin to hold back the cry of her second release.

Suddenly the music lowered, and the driver hollered, "We're here."

우신 cleared his throat and responded, 'Thank you."

He slid his fingers out of her, coated in her pleasure, as she climbed off him, zipping her pants up and quickly moved to the door. He adjusted himself, sitting for a little while longer, trying to calm himself down.

Once she was out of the car and walking away, 우신 made his way toward the exit of the car, dragging his backpack with him, when the driver cleared his throat and said, "Have fun."

A blush crept onto 우신's face but, if he was being honest, he wasn't ashamed of what they had done or the fact that they had gotten caught. Throwing inhibitions to the wind was something he hadn't thought to try in his quest to find the inspiration he needed for the creation of CLAR1T's new album. But also in the journey to find himself again. To find what he had lost when the pressure of becoming an idol became all-consuming.

He knew it sounded crazy that an act of exhibitionism would spark such an epiphany, but it wasn't the act itself. It was who it was with and what she had been able to bring out in him throughout the night. The exhibitionism was icing on the cake.

He bowed his head to the driver and leapt out of the car, closing the door; it quickly sped away. As he walked over to Bridgette, who was fiddling with her keys, he pulled his cap off quickly to fix his hair back into its bun. When he finally did reach her, he noticed she was refusing to glance directly at him. Was she embarrassed by what they had done? Ashamed?

"누나, are you upset about what happened back there? If I went too far, you can tell me. I can get too in my head sometimes and, well…I've been told I can be too much." He nodded to where the car had been. He wanted to take a step closer to her, but he didn't want to see the potential negative reaction of her backing away from him, so he kept his feet planted firmly on the concrete.

Her eyes finally met his, wide with an unreadable expression.

"What? No. No, that's not it. I'm just…" She trailed off, dropping her hands to her side, the keys jingling in the eerie silence of the street. A street he had walked before. How could a street in a city he'd only been in for three days be familiar? And that's when he saw where they stood. In front of her café.

"Why are we back here?" he asked.

"I live above the shop." She pointed to the second floor of the building, where he could see some dim lights behind what looked like flowy opaque curtains.

"Your commute to work must be such a hassle." He laughed and saw only a quick smile from her. Something was off. "Bridgette, what's wrong?"

"I'm a fangirl, 우 신," she finally blurted out. "A fangirl of you and your group. I have pictures and posters of you on one of my walls. I have your album and collect all the versions of your photocards. And at my age, people tell me I need to settle down. Get married, maybe even have a kid or two. But here I am following a boy group."

"I'm twenty-seven and in that 'boy' group," he retorted.

"Sure, but you're not used to walking into a stranger's home that has your face on their wall." She swiped at her forehead.

"You'd be surprised how often that has happened." He chuckled, doing anything to try to quell her anxiety.

"우 신…" She trailed off, still obviously nervous about him seeing her place.

"How about I be the judge of whether I find your place too

much or not?" He finally stepped closer to her, grabbing her hands, clammy due to her overthinking.

As he squeezed her hands in encouragement, she let out a sigh, followed by a quick nod before turning toward her café and leading him to a side entrance.

CHAPTER FIVE

Bridgette was a bumbling mess trying to put her key into the lock of her door. Not only because 우 신 was standing behind her waiting to be let into her apartment, but because her mind replayed short snippets of what they had done in the car.

She was shocked at how his inhibitions had deteriorated throughout the night. From when he first walked into her shop, covered up from head to toe and softly whispering his order, to now where he had just finger fucked her in the back seat of a car with not a care in the world if the driver caught them or not. His whole attitude changed, and she started to think it was something he needed.

And the power of those orgasms he gave her had her thinking he was something she needed as well.

When she finally heard the click of her door unlocking, panic set in stronger than when she had confessed that she was nervous for him to see her apartment. She pushed the door open and stood to the side, letting him enter the stairwell leading up to her place. She watched as he began his ascension, but he stopped and turned back toward her.

"Are you going to stay there the whole night?" He came back down the stairs and pulled her into the entryway, her hand on the knob pulling the door closed behind her and her body pressed against his. When she looked up, his eyes had that lustful hunger they had before they'd climbed into the car.

"우 신?" She didn't know why his name came out as a question, but he seemed desperate to answer.

"I don't think I can wait until we get up there," he growled. His hand gripped the back of her head and pulled her up to crash his lips onto hers. Instantly her arms wrapped around his neck, as his hand left the back of her head and moved down and around the button of her jeans. She had no time to think before he had unzipped them once again. He pulled both her jeans and panties down, and as they scraped across her ass, she whimpered. His nails scratched her legs before his hands moved back up her thighs and one slipped between her folds, causing her to grip his shoulders harder. Her hips ground against his fingers.

"You're dripping, 누나. I can't wait until I'm inside you," he breathed against her lips.

I'm about to have sex in the entryway to my apartment.

She wasn't questioning it, rather she was processing that this man, this idol, was so desperate for her he couldn't take another step without being with her. And it invigorated her that she was so desired by him. She unwrapped her hands from his neck, bringing them to his waistband; following his lead, she pushed his sweats and boxer briefs down.

While she had felt his cock, she hadn't seen it. When she broke their lips apart so she could catch a glimpse of what was about to be inside her, her eyes went wide. When it had pressed up against her and even when she'd had it cupped in her hand, it didn't feel as large as what she currently was gazing upon. Was it possible for it to grow that much larger?

"I have a 콘돔* in my bag," he said between his panting breaths. He let go of her for a second and shimmied the bag off his shoul-

---

* 콘돔 – kondom - condom

ders before pulling it around in front of him, blocking her view of his cock.

"That wasn't what I was thinking about, but very smart thinking on your part." She was panting too, and as a breeze blew across her legs, she realized her pants were down to her knees. As she tried to pull them back up, a hand grabbed her wrist to stop her.

"Don't pull them up," he commanded.

"네?" she breathed.

"I told you I can't wait. So don't you dare pull them back up." He retrieved the condom from his bag, brought the corner to his mouth and ripped open the packaging.

Her breath caught as she watched him pull the condom from the wrapper and slide it down his cock. The long, hard cock that she never in a million years imagined she would not only be seeing, but touching, and having inside her, making her cum. She shivered at the thought of what it was going to feel like having him inside her.

"I'm still allowed to tell you what I want, right?" His previous commanding tone had disappeared and was replaced with a nervous one.

The many changes she'd seen in his demeanor throughout the night were coming full circle in front of her. From the initial anxiously quiet guy who entered her café, to the one who came to her rescue and powerfully scared away drunkards. From the one who opened up about his depression and anxiety, to the one who helped her deliver and plate pastries at the women's shelter. And finally from the man who kissed her in a bar and became an exhibitionist in the ride back to her place, to returning to that anxiously nervous guy who walked into her café.

She cupped his cheek, his eyes sparkling when they met hers — as he watched her, her heart warmed. "You can tell me everything."

She had realized that certain things she said changed his manner. Her last statement was one of them. His shoulders relaxed, his Adam's apple bobbed, his eyes gave her their undivided attention. He tossed his bag to the side as his eyes roamed all around her face.

"There is so much I want to do with you " He brought his hands to her bare hips, pulling her naked half to his. She let out a small squeak of surprise but smiled at him as her heart raced at all the possibilities his statement held. With a smirk stretching up one side of his face, he spun her around, his hand spread wide just above where her body was screaming for him to be.

Soft lips caressed the shell of her ear, followed by his teeth scraping gently before he whispered, "Bend over and grab the railing."

With a shiver, she silently, and rather happily, obeyed his orders. Her hands gripped the cold, hard metal railing as her ass pressed against his thighs, his cock pressing just above on her lower back. His hands roamed around her waist, down her thighs, and back up toward her ass, where he grabbed two handfuls and pushed himself against her.

"Hold on tight, 누나." His voice had returned to that commanding and demanding tone that made her wet. She gripped the railing tighter which earned a, "Good, 누나."

Every time he said that word her body had a reaction. She would get all warm and fuzzy, then turned on and dripping desperate for him to be inside her. The word, coming from his mouth, had quickly become her kryptonite.

He spread her ass cheeks and his cock slid between them until finding her entrance that was begging for him.

"I can feel you clenching around just my tip. You want me that badly?" he asked as he pressed the tip of his cock inside her, holding it there, awaiting her response.

"응*." She nodded furiously. She wanted him inside her and she pushed herself onto him a bit, which made him grab and squeeze her hips. With no warning, his cock thrust fully into her, causing her to let out a loud gasp. He filled her, stretched her, and it was the most delicious feeling. Her legs shook, getting weak, but she had to stand strong so she could continue to feel him inside her. She pressed her ass back into him, filling her with every last bit.

The thrill of being in the entryway, bent over holding onto the

---

* 응 – eung - yes

railing while the idol of her dreams was taking her from behind had her already teetering on the edge of another orgasm. The third he would have given her so far. He pulled out to pound back in, and she let out another gasp. She bit the inside of her cheek because, while they were technically inside her apartment, the street was still just outside. The door wasn't soundproof, as she could sometimes hear people walking by when she took the stairs to leave her apartment and go to the café.

His hand reached around her waist and his fingers slid to her clit, making her already shaking legs buckle.

"Keep your stunning ass up, 누나." His other hand gripped hard onto one of her ass cheeks as he continued to relentlessly pound his cock into her.

"I-I-I ca-can't." She got out the few words she could before continuing to bite the inside of her cheek.

"You're ready to cum already?" His tone was laced with amusement. Clearly happy with how quickly he could get her on the edge of her climax, ready to fly. She nodded vigorously. "We will cum together on my count. 알았어?*"

Her head dropped, and she noticed she could see their bodies meeting. His thigh muscles tensing with every thrust into her, his hand between her legs playing with her clit, and her own pleasure coating her inner thighs. It was too much, she couldn't control it. She shook her head, trying to hold on for his count to cum. But as she continued to watch their bodies meeting, her body had other plans. She reached euphoria, shaking with tingling sensations running to every end of her body before her vision went black.

"You don't like following orders, huh?' His voice brought her back down to earth. His fingers left her clit and he pulled out of her. An emptiness set in.

"미안해," she said between pants. "I tried. I really did."

A rush of cold air hit her backside, and she looked over her shoulder to see him pulling up his pants and grabbing his bag from

---

* 알았어? - al-ass-eo? – understood?

the floor. She straightened up, and when she went to pull her pants back up, her legs were like jelly, and she stumbled slightly.

His reaction time was unmatched, and his hand wrapped around her waist to keep her up.

"고마워," she let out breathlessly. He nodded, but before she could ask if she had ruined the night by what she did, he bent down, his arm gripped her waist harder, and his other arm moved behind her knees—suddenly she was in the air. She yelped, "뭐 하는 거 야?*"

He continued to move in silence and began to climb the stairs. She wanted to squirm out of his hold, but that could've ended horribly for both of them. She chose to wrap her arms around his neck and wait until they got to the top landing, where she could unlock her door. Again, nerves sank in about him seeing her wall of CLAR1T merchandise, but he continued to act unfazed.

Once at the top he put her down, his hand staying around her waist to keep her back against his chest. She wanted to bask in his warmth forever. It was like nothing she had ever experienced with a partner. He was the summer sun setting her body ablaze. Bridgette was happy to have moments she could remember that would always only be attributed to 우신. Things she could call her own that no other fan could. That moment was one of them.

"Your legs better now?" he whispered against her ear. His lips again grazed the shell, making her shiver and grab his hand that stayed on her waist. She responded by pushing her butt into his groin. His hot breath, through his silently strong laugh, cascaded down her neck.

She finally got the key in the door, hearing the click of the latch unlocking, she pushed it in. *This is it.*

---

* 뭐 하는 거야? - mwo haneun geoya? – what are you doing?

CHAPTER SIX

신 stood behind Bridgette, waiting for her to walk through her front door. Instead, she pushed it open and turned sideways in order for him to enter first. He had only taken two steps in, and he was hit with the scent of baked goods. The savory yeastiness of bread mixed with the sweet sugariness of cookies. It smelled exactly like Bridgette. A scent he wanted ingrained in his memory for days, weeks, months, years to come. Her scent, the café scent, her apartment scent caused more ice to melt away from that tundra in his chest.

The place was spacious, covering the entirety of the café below. It had similar high walls; however, there were only two rather large windows facing out to the street instead of the floor-to-ceiling windows of the café. But it was filled with so much more: Bridgette's memories. It was lived in. From the deep brown suede couch that he could see her seat impressions on, to the TV hanging on the wall surrounded by picture frames of memories and shelves of small plants and books. The lighting was soft, cascading caramel-like light through the open space.

He was jealous of the place. Their dorms at the company had been bare bones. At first, he thought it was because they were a small company that couldn't afford much. But when they were bought by LML Entertainment, a massive corporation, he thought things would've changed. They didn't. He then came to the conclusion it was in order to keep them focused on debuting and nothing else.

They had been able to get their own places much earlier than most newly debuted groups, between the financial smarts of Minhwa getting them out of their debt to the company faster than most and their instant international success. But since they went into training with very little and debuted with very little, there wasn't much for him to put into his new place. He was thinking about creating a small studio space so he would be able to produce in peace, but they were already announcing their US tour before he could even put his bed together.

우신 walked farther into the room, and as he took in all of the space, he caught a glimpse of himself. Sitting on a bookshelf was their album, his photocards framed along with the other members, sitting beside their light stick, the L1TBONG. On the wall beside the bookshelf was the poster from the album and his postcard along with Minhwa's beside it, hung nicely in frames. He made his way over to the shelf, smiling about how nervous Bridgette had been for him to see her fanaticism.

He heard the clank of her keys on the sideboard behind him, and she continued to stand hidden from his view. 우신 wondered if she was trying to avoid his reaction to her place or the reaction to her collection.

"Your apartment is very nice." He smiled, finally turning to face her. He pointed to the wall that held her memorabilia. "This is my favorite part."

He laughed and watched her shoulders drop in relief as a tiny smile crept onto her lips. Lips he wanted back on his sooner rather than later.

"화장실 어디 있어?*" he asked, needing to get the condom off

---

* 화장실 어디 있어? - hwajangsil eodi isso갈까요? – Where is the bathroom?

his still rather rock-hard cock that was currently tucked in his waistband.

"Through the door on the right and then the first door on the left is the bathroom," she directed as she made her way toward the kitchen.

He walked to the door, and when he entered the room, he was surprised to see it was her bedroom. What didn't surprise him was that it was a lived-in room with its large bed covered in a colorful floral comforter, and in the corner was a chair with a pile of clothes beside a large mirror. The room had that similar soft tanned lighting from the living room, warming him.

He walked to the bathroom, and as he opened the door he heard Bridgette holler, "Can I get you anything to drink?"

"Whatever you're having," he responded as he heard the clinking of bottles and glasses. He moved quickly once in the bathroom to get the condom off and make his way back to the living room.

"소주* sound good?" she asked softly as he reentered. She held up shot glasses and two bottles of 소주 in her hands.

He smirked, laughing at the traditional Korean drink and dipping his head as he reached for the 소주 and glasses. He made his way toward the couch, choosing to sit in front of it on the area rug that was nicely cushioned. Clanking the glasses down in front of him, he grabbed the bottle and flicked it to make the 소주 tornado before hitting the bottom of the bottle to his elbow and twisting the cap open. The scent of familiarity made him feel at home in Bridgette's environment. He poured both glasses and slid one to his side to get her to join him. She plopped down beside him, snatching up the drink and clinking it with his.

"짠†," they said simultaneously, tipping their heads back, and the liquor poured down his throat. That familiar pleasurable burn as it traveled through his body had him releasing a throaty groan of

---

* 소주 – soju - soju
† 짠 – jjan - cheers

enjoyment. He watched her bite back the burn of the alcohol before she puckered her lips to let out a breathy exhale.

"I forgot how strong the non-flavored one is." She laughed as she lifted the bottle to pour him and herself another shot. They once again clinked and brought the glasses to their lips.

He put his down on the coffee table as she slammed hers down hard. She was about to pour another two shots, but he put his hand over the two glasses to stop her.

"Are you trying to get us wasted?" He laughed, but in all seriousness, he wanted to know why she was trying to drink so quickly.

"아니, 근데*..." She trailed off and, with a deep sigh and her face stoic, her eyes focused on him. "너 괜찮아?†"

Such an odd question to ask me. He laughed at the randomness. He had felt the most free he had in years. And it was thanks to her. He was more than okay, he was...wait. His smile faltered. He met her gaze and saw a glistening that hadn't been there a second ago.

"너 괜찮아?" she asked again, her voice cracking.

Why was his heart racing? His breath becoming unsteady? His hands suddenly going clammy? When was the last time someone had asked him that? And when was the last time he had given a *real* answer to it?

Bridgette shifted her body closer to him and reached up to take the baseball cap off his head, her first *real* look at him with nothing blocking his features, without passion fogging her vision. Her hand went to his cheek, and the calm he had felt started to seep back into his body. His breathing steadied. His hands instinctively reached for her to pull her closer. So close he had her on his lap and buried his head into the crook of her shoulder. He had already cried once on her, what was one more time? It had been cathartic the first time. This time he sensed a small amount of healing. More of that cold interior was warming, melting, bringing him back to a version of himself he had missed and worried he would never see again.

---

* 아니, 근데 - ani, geunde – not, but
† 너 괜찮아? - neo gwaenchanh-a? – are you ok? (more pressing than simply gwaen-chanh-a? Adding the neo(you) is stronger.)

56

His sobs were silent as she held him, rubbed his back, kissed his temple. He drew his head back to look at her and found tears streaming down her face as well. He cupped her cheek like she had previously done to him and wiped away the tears.

"I'm going to be. And so are you." He answered her question between every breath through his trembling lips. Her mouth drew downward in a frown of agreement as opposed to sadness. She moved in his lap to straddle him, similarly to in the car.

She reached behind his head, and he felt a tug on the hair tie that had been holding his bun in place. She pulled the tie free from his hair. He mimicked her, reaching up to her hair to pull out her hair tie, allowing the beautiful strawberry-blonde hair to cascade down her shoulders. He ran his fingers through tresses that reminded him of the softness of silk.

Her hands went to either side of his head, running her fingers through his hair and making him shiver, goosebumps rising all across his skin. She traced down his neck and to his chest, where his heart thudded so hard, he knew she felt it against her palm. She slowly dropped her hands from his body and reached down to the hem of her shirt, lifting it up and over her head.

He inhaled sharply, taking in the beauty of her soft, creamy skin. He ran his fingers up and down every inch she offered him. He swallowed loudly as he watched how her skin reacted to his hands. When he grazed her stomach, she tensed but her head fell back. When they moved up to her bra-covered breasts, she sighed and he saw a rose-colored flush across her chest. She reached behind her and he watched as her bra loosened its hold before falling between them. Her breasts—her gorgeous, stunning, mouthwateringly perfect breasts—fell from their cage, and he was hungry to bury his face in them.

He let go of her to remove his own shirt, wanting to feel the warmth of her body against his. This moment was vastly different from their last two in the night. Those were filled with hunger and lust. He was pleasure-seeking and he was getting it from their exhibitionism instead of his initial plan of the night, which was drowning in alcohol.

But that moment, their naked chests against one another was them stripping each other bare—not only literally but emotionally. Sharing their fears, their worries, their dread, their dreams, their hopefulness, their happiness.

He reached up, his lips softly pressing against hers, igniting their physical desperation to be near one another. She moaned into his mouth before his lips left hers, unintentionally following her tears. The salt mixing with her sweet skin as he moved down her throat to her breast. He had been thinking of having his mouth on her body since he had tried making a move on her hours ago, in the café on the floor. She leaned back to allow him more access to her breasts. As his lips wrapped around one of her nipples, it hardened instantly and he grabbed her other one as she ground her hips down onto his lap.

"정말 아름다워*." He heavily breathed out before moving his lips across her chest to give his attention to her other breast. She didn't speak, but her body told him everything he wanted to know. She stroked her hands through his hair, grabbing fistfuls every time his tongue flicked at her nipple. Her back arched, pressing her chest to his mouth as his hand traced up and down her spine. Her hips ground into him when he gripped one of her ass cheeks. Every movement told him that she felt as beautiful inside and out as he had meant his praise to mean.

She pulled her body away from his, both of them catching their breath, their eyes meeting. She smiled gently, pressing her lips to his.

"I promise. I promise this time I can follow your instructions," she swore before bringing her lips to his once again. Reaching her hand down between them, she palmed his rock-hard cock. He knew she was referring to cumming at his command, but with her promise he had something else in mind.

"Can you?" His rhetorical question was met with a wickedly sexy grin and several quick nods, which made him chuckle. "Get naked."

She got off his lap, standing to pull her pants and underwear off

---

* 정말 아름다워 - jeongmal aleumdawo – you're really beautiful

and tossing them to the side. Seeing her fully nude standing in front of him. Her hourglass-shaped curves, her beautiful porcelain-like skin resembled a sculpture. An art piece that should be worshipped. And he planned to.

He reached out to grab her hand. "Get on your bed and I will be right there."

Her eyes were questioning, she bit the corner of her bottom lip, and with her free hand, she tried to cover parts of her beautiful naked body.

"걱정마*," he reassured her. "I'll be right behind you. I just want to grab something from my bag."

She dropped her hand from his, slowly walking to her bedroom and giving him an enjoyable view of her backside before disappearing through the doorway. He scrambled to his feet and grabbed his bag, ripping open the largest section and pulling out what he knew was going to bring their night to an orgasmic crescendo.

---

* 걱정마 – geogjeongma – don't worry

CHAPTER SEVEN

Bridgette climbed onto her bed, staring at the ceiling, nervous that when he'd seen her fully naked, he wanted to run for the hills. Her breasts weren't perky, she had some cellulite on her thighs, her skincare routine included special eye creams to keep the crow's feet away as well as other concoctions for her laugh lines. Koreans did have a high beauty standard that she knew she didn't fit. As her mind raced, a loud thud from beside her bed brought her mind back into the room.

She turned to see 우 신 opening the window, and a cool breeze made her curtains dance about and her nipples harden. She leaned up on her elbows, wondering why he had opened the window when they were about to have sex. Wouldn't people outside possibly hear them?

But then he turned toward her and she got a perfect view of his broad shoulders, muscular pecks, and abs that looked like perfectly shaped squares of a chocolate bar; she was ready to break off a piece. She no longer cared what reason he had for opening the window.

He was an Adonis-like figure. So beautifully mesmerizing he didn't seem real. And yet he was, and he was walking toward her prone naked body. She got to enjoy the V shape of his hips, moving ever so slowly, leading down to the only garments still left on his body. She desperately waited, feeling the need for him between her legs, for his next move. He sat on the edge of the bed, his back to her, staring out of the window he had just opened.

She took the initiative to sit up on her knees, approaching from behind to straddle him between her thighs, her chest against his back. He released a deep sigh, his head falling forward as he ran his hand through his hair. Her fingers traced up his back and scratched back down, and she caught a shiver through him, and…did he growl?

"누나," he moaned as she continued to explore his torso. She added her lips to the mix, finding his skin was creamy soft. There was a saltiness that she gathered was a mix of performing earlier that evening, helping her run errands throughout the night, and most definitely fingering her in the car and their encounter in the entryway of her home.

She pressed her body tighter to his, her hands moving to explore his chest. Her lips found their comfort in his neck and also gently nipping his earlobe. Another shudder ran through him, followed by what she could confirm was in fact a growl. It empowered her that it was possible she could make a man like him wild like that.

He grabbed one of her hands from his chest and turned his head so his lips met hers. His lips might've been on the thinner side, but from all their kissing they had swollen slightly, and she relished nipping at his bottom lip.

"Lie back on the bed," he commanded, dropping her hand to stand and watch her do as he said.

She obeyed immediately, happily moving herself to the center of the bed and falling back, her head hitting the pillows. She was again on display to him. Her nerves had come back as his eyes raked over her body. They paused several times, and she saw a glimmer in his eyes with every pause.

"Can I ask what you're thinking about?" she whispered.

His eyes roamed back up to meet hers and held a hungered lust when he smiled at her. "I'm thinking of all the things I want to do to you, with you, for you."

Those words took her breath away. She was speechless at his confession. But it also excited her for what was about to happen. He pulled down his boxer briefs and pants, his cock jumping to attention now that they were both fully on display to one another. Her view of him as an Adonis didn't change. He still looked like something unobtainable, yet there he was, very much in reach of her.

Climbing onto the bed, he reached for something at the bottom corner. How had she not noticed he put something on the bed?

"뭐야?*" She pointed to what he held in his hand.

"이거†…" He lifted the item in his hand. The big reveal was the headphones she had seen him wearing in her café earlier in the evening.

"헤드폰‡?" She stared at them, confused as to how those would be necessary for what they were about to do.

He nodded toward the open window. Her eyes followed, still not grasping what he was trying to accomplish.

"If you heard yourself, you would stop making any kind of noise. You held back in the kitchen, in the bar, in the car, even in front of your home." He placed the headphones on her head, and suddenly the world was completely silent. He pulled off one side for her to hear again. "I want you to scream in pleasure. I want you to not be ashamed of it. And I want people to hear how much you're enjoying yourself."

"Those were all public places, 우신," she countered.

"나를 봐§," he said, as his fingers traced down her neck, between her breasts, down her stomach, and made their way down to her most sensitive spot. Her center that had been dying to have him inside her once again. "If I put my fingers here."

---

* 뭐야? - mwoya? – what?

† 이거 – iego - this

‡ 헤드폰 – hedeupon - headphone

§ 나를 봐 - naleul bwa – look at me

63

They slipped between her folds, finding her clit instantly. She arched her body in surprise.

"And my mouth here," he whispered close to her ear before using his tongue to flick her earlobe into his mouth, his lips gently sucking before moving down her neck. She choked on air as her body came alive from his touch. His fingers circled her clit, his lips sucked on her collarbone, and she bit down on her bottom lip.

"See?" He pulled his head back, their eyes meeting. "You hold back."

"I—" She wanted to argue, but he was right.

"If you can't hear yourself, I wonder if that will let you set yourself free." He put the headphone back on her ear, and she returned to the silence of her own mind.

He raised an eyebrow, silently asking if he could continue. She gave a quick nod in agreement, and he wasted no time as his fingers circled her clit again. His mouth left hot open-mouthed kisses down her neck to her chest, where he sucked on each of her nipples before continuing south.

He kissed each side of her hipbone, and she watched him intensely as he stared up at her. A sinful, sinister smile appeared on his lips before they met his finger between her legs. She shot her hips up to meet him as her hand went into his hair. It was coarse but fluffy and somewhat sticky from the extra-strong hairspray they used for performing. She tugged on it, but his tongue probed into her, and suddenly the tugging away became pushing him against her. His hands went to her thighs, placing them on his shoulders as his mouth devoured her. She felt him speaking, but she obviously couldn't hear him, and she wanted to. She moved to push one side of the headphones but before she could, his hand went to her breast and his fingers pinched her nipple.

She let out a sound, unable to hear it, but she looked down to see him between her legs, eyes on hers as he shook his head, telling her not to remove the headphones. While she wanted to disobey and hear his voice, he pinched her nipple again like he knew what she was thinking and shook his head again.

With 우신's hair tickling her inner thighs, his mouth feasting on her, and his fingers both playing with her clit and pinching her nipples, she knew if she disobeyed it would all stop. She removed her hand from the headphone to grab his hand on her breast and squeezed hard to show him she liked what he was doing. Her hips ground to meet his mouth as she held onto his hair.

She could feel her release building. And she sensed he could too. His motions became quicker. Rapid circles of her clit, his tongue pushing in and out before swiping and sucking to taste her pleasure. She moaned. She knew she did but she could barely hear it. She felt a smile on his lips and again he spoke, and it frustrated her that she was unable to hear it. She wanted to hear him.

She suddenly realized why he had done what he did. He wanted to hear her enjoy herself. He wanted to know that what he was doing made her feel good. And with that in mind, she kept the headphones right where they were and continued to rock her hips on his face. She let her mouth hang open, allowing herself to make whatever sounds her body chose.

She was almost to the height of her climax when he pulled away. His fingers weren't rubbing her clit, his mouth wasn't on her cunt, and his hand wasn't squeezing and pinching her breast and nipple. Her legs weren't draped on his shoulders. She raised her head to see him sitting up on his knees ripping another condom wrapper with his teeth and sliding it down his cock.

She internally screamed, *Let him finish this time, you dingbat.*

He spread her legs wider, wrapped an arm around her waist to lift her hips as he dropped down to sink into her.

She *knew* she let out the loudest moan she probably ever had. Seeing the wide smile on 우신's face, she knew it was exactly what he wanted to hear with his first pump into her.

He slowly dropped down, his hands on either side of her head, his eyes appearing to read her enjoyment. She wrapped her arms around his neck, one hand snaking into his hair again, as she brought his lips to hers. He began pumping in and out hard, making her head almost hit her headboard with every thrust into her.

Her legs went around his waist, and he used that to flip them around while holding her on top. He was now even deeper inside her, which she didn't think was possible. She looked down at him and he began to mouth something.

"올- 올-올라-올라타*."

She tried to follow the movements of his mouth, sounding it out as best she could. He nodded when she had said the whole phrase, but she didn't know what the words meant.

He moved his hips, making her grab the top of her headboard as he hit the right spot. She gazed back down at him, and he mouthed again. This time in English.

Ride me.

Needing no more instruction, she lifted up onto her knees before sliding back down onto his cock. She ground around in a circle, causing him to grab her hips, digging his nails into her flesh. She again could feel herself moan, uncaring about how loud she was. She knew he enjoyed hearing her and she enjoyed seeing him being excited by her. She began to bounce on his cock, and she could feel pressure building in her.

She wouldn't cum first. Absolutely not. She had already gotten her fair share of orgasms. Once he came, she would ride out another one of her own highs. As she bounced, his hips met her thrusts with such force, he got deeper than she ever had enjoyed. His hands on her hips were digging harder, and she saw his abs clenching as well as his neck muscles tensing. She traced her fingers down his neck, following one straining muscle down to his pecks. Then she gave back the pleasure he'd given her and pinched his nipples.

That was his breaking point. Suddenly there was no more rhythm to his pumping. He was a man possessed. But with his quickness he kept hitting the right spot, and she could feel her moans getting louder. She continued to hold back her orgasm.

His erratic pumps, her grinding to meet him rubbing her clit as his cock was hitting all the right places inside her, trying to hold back her orgasm was torture. That's when the headphones were ripped from her head and she heard his command.

---

* 올라타 – ollata – literally means 'get on' but in this sense it means 'ride me'

66

"니가 받고 있는 스트레스 나한테 다 풀어보라고!*. Scream for me."

The gruffness of his voice did it. Bridgette screamed out his name into the void, as her vision went black and her body shattered into a million pieces. Electric shocks ran through her whole body, and she felt herself pulse around his cock.

His hips slowed their brutal pace, becoming slow juts in and out, and when she finally returned from the bliss of her high, he turned them so that she collapsed beside him. He slipped out of her with ease and got up, walking into her bathroom. When he came back, the condom was off and he held a towel.

It was like he'd lived there for years, rather than it being his first time in her apartment. He laid down beside her again and began cleaning up the mess she had made. The rough towel on her sensitive slit made her let out a small squeak. He apologized softly and kissed her forehead before dropping the towel to the side of the bed and pulling her naked, sweaty, satiated body to his.

Her breathing was slowing back to a normal pace, and when she opened her eyes, she saw him staring at her with the happiest dopey smile on his face.

"뭐야?" She covered her face, embarrassed he was looking at her with such adoration she didn't think she deserved.

"고마워," he whispered as he pulled her hands off her face and brought them to his lips, kissing them gently.

"Why are you thanking me?" She giggled, burying her head in his neck.

"For letting me be me. Not the idol version of me or the producer version of me. Just plain old 우신." He kissed the side of her head. She loved how gentle he was after what he had just done to her; the switch had been instant. She leaned back to give him a sweet peck on the lips.

"I wouldn't do exhibitionism with just plain old anybody. But I'm happy I got to experience it with you. With just your everyday

---

* 니가 받고 있는 스트레스 나한테 다 풀어보라고!- solijilleobwa! niga badgo issneun seuteuleseu nahante da pul-eobolago!- Take out all your stress on me.

우 신." She snuggled against his chest, kissing him and tasting the extra bit of salt from their vigorous activity.

"우 신, I know it's impossible for this to be more than tonight," she whispered. When she received no argument or protest, she continued, "I want you to know how happy I am to have met you and spent this time together. I hope you create more amazing music for you and CLAR1T, and I hope you realize how loved you are."

She still received no response. When she moved her head to get a look at his face, she saw he was sound asleep with a dreamy smile on his lips. She reached up to softly push away strands of his hair that had fallen in his face. He twitched, and his arm wrapped around her suddenly, pulling her more tightly to his chest.

"잘 자 우 신*." She snuggled back into his chest and closed her eyes. She knew she would have to be up in two hours to start baking, but his warmth lulled her safely to sleep.

---

* 잘 자 우 신 - jal ja u sin - sleep well Woo Shin

CHAPTER EIGHT

우
신 woke up to light pouring through the open window, where the sound of cars driving on the street one story down made him grab his phone to check the time—8 a.m.

He shot up in the bed to wake Bridgette and tell her he needed to leave, but she wasn't beside him. He scanned the room but saw no trace of her. Calming himself, he took a deep breath and was rewarded with the smell of coffee and baked goods.

She must be downstairs.

He got dressed, packing his headphones in his bag before making his way down to the café. Once downstairs he saw an open door in her apartment entryway leading into the café. He walked through the door to see everything as they'd left it last night, however there was an 아야on the counter, and he could hear music coming from the kitchen.

Not just any music, but music he had written. He smiled and pushed through the swinging door to see Bridgette dancing around the counter where trays of different pastries sat. She walked to the oven and pulled out a tray full of loaves of빵*. He watched from the doorway, seeing her hips sway, her lips mouthing the words, and her hands skillfully slicing the bread.

"I could get used to waking up to this every morning," he finally said, not wanting to continue intruding on what looked to be a morning ritual.

She jumped back from the 빵 and tossed the knife onto the counter. When she saw him, she let out a sigh of relief and shut off the music.

"I thought I had accidently unlocked the front door and someone came in!" She clutched her chest.

"Are you not open right now?" he asked. She was a café after all.

"Not open today. I have one rest day a week." She laughed. "Not much rest though. I usually prep some of the longer-lasting breads and pastries for tomorrow's morning rush. The coffee out there is for you though."

"고마워 ." He dipped his head and went back out to the front to pour himself some coffee. When he came back she had returned to cutting the 빵.

"누나…" He trailed off. He had to leave, though he didn't want to. He wished he could stay the rest of the day with her, but they had a flight that night to the next city.

"I packed you some pastries to bring back with you." She picked up a large brown paper bag. "I would love it if you shared them with your groupmates."

She gave him a warm smile as she handed him the bag. He was about to make a remark about her wanting him to give them specifically to Minhwa when she stood on her tiptoes and softly pressed her lips to his. He took the bag from her hands, putting it back on the counter before wrapping her in his arms and making sure to give her a thorough kiss.

"어젯밤†…" He kept his arms around her waist as he looked

---

* 빵 – ppang- bread
† 어젯밤 – eojesbam – last night

down at her and saw her stunningly cheerful smile, her cheeks lit up bright red.

"I had fun." She giggled and dropped her head to his chest.

"저도*," he agreed, pulling her closer to him, soaking in every last ounce of warmth he could get. He inhaled deeply, trying to commit her scent to memory.

"You have to go, don't you?" she mumbled against his chest before pulling her face away to stare up at his. Her big puppy dog eyes and a small pout had him questioning if he should leave. But he knew what he had to do. He nodded.

"Bridgette… 누나…" His mind raced with all the things he wanted to say to her, but none of them seemed to be able to reach his lips. As he struggled to speak, she lifted her arm and showed him her wrist, where a small black hair tie sat.

"Do you mind if I keep this?" she asked. "I would like at least one tangible thing to remind me of you. The real 우신."

He could see her eyes had reddened and her lips trembled, and suddenly the entire wall in his chest came crumbling down. He grabbed her wrist, holding the hair tie in place, and pressed a kiss to her pulse as well as the tie. He felt her pulse quicken on his lips before he began to kiss up her arm.

"우신…" she moaned.

"응." He was too distracted by her to form anything more than an acknowledgement of his name. He reached her neck and she pulled away.

"우신, you need to go. Your groupmates are probably looking for you. And you need to head to your next tour stop." She pulled her arm out of his hold and took several steps back from him. The wall that had just crumbled was already rebuilding itself. He couldn't look at her. His head dropped and he grabbed the bag of pastries, his coffee, and made his way to the door.

"잠깐만!†" she shouted and came running around to stop him.

"You're right, 누나. I need to leave." He held back his emotions.

---

* 저도 – jeodo – me too
† 잠깐만 – jamkkanman – wait a second

He had already opened up to her more than he probably should have. She could go and tell everyone his secrets. They never talked about what would happen the next morning.

"I need to say one more thing before you leave." Her eyes frantically scanned over his face, waiting for him to give her the go-ahead to speak. Which he did.

She took a deep breath and began, "우 신, you are beyond talented. You have made millions of fans fall in love with your group. *You* did that. Your music did that. You have worked so hard, you have brought so many smiles to people who didn't think they could smile again."

Her breathing was quickening. "I needed you to hear that one more time before you left. And I also need you to hear that…" She paused, looking uncertain about what she planned to say next. Instead of words, she grabbed his shirt and pulled him down to kiss him. He pressed his lips to hers once more. He needed it. He wanted so much more from her. Mentally and physically he felt safe with her, and the fact that he'd questioned that for a second made him feel horrible.

She pulled away from the kiss and enfolded her arms around his waist; instinctively he wrapped his rather full hands around her neck, burying her head in his chest. When he could hear her mumble something, he released her slightly.

"What was that?"

"I need you to hear that the café is always open for you. Always." She gave him one more strong squeeze before dropping her arms from around him. "You really do need to go though."

"I will be back. 약속해*." He kissed her forehead, sealing the promise he made.

---

* 약속해 – yagsoghae – I promise

CHAPTER NINE

Four months later...
Bridgette hadn't heard from 우신 since he left the morning after their encounter. She had put her number in the bag of pastries with a note telling him to feel free to reach out whenever he needed. Clearly he didn't need to, or possibly didn't want to. She didn't expect him to either. He was an idol after all. His life was scheduled down to the second. And with how much more popular they had become since their tour and promotions in the US, she was sure he had even less time.

That also made her worry about him. Was he eating? Getting a decent night's rest? Was he having bad thoughts again? Did he have someone to talk to?

Those questions crossed her mind fairly often.

As the true CLARvoyant she was, she had been following their travels since her clandestine meeting with 우신. She knew they had arrived back in Korea a month ago. She also saw that 우신 and 성준 had come back to the US to work on some special projects. She hoped that maybe he would stop by the shop, but after a week of him being in the country with zero contact, she felt all hope of seeing him again was lost. She had come to terms with the fact that she was a moment in his life that he had moved on from, and she would have to move on as well.

She started the cleanup of the kitchen like any regular night while Amanda stayed out front with one or two night owls. She could hear the jingle of the front entrance, which she assumed was one of the patrons leaving. That was until the swinging door squeaked open and Amanda's head popped in.

"Hey Bridg, someone came in wanting to speak to the owner." She had a nervous air about her.

"Now?" She looked to the clock on the wall—it was nearly 2 a.m. "Can you ask them to come back tomorrow at a reasonable hour?" Bridgette wiped her hands on the towel and then on her apron. She had a lot to get done before she would be able to close, and she didn't have time to deal with a random customer.

"He seems pretty adamant about speaking to you now." Amanda's nervousness had Bridgette worried. Was this man disgruntled? Drunk?

"Alright, I'm coming." Bridgette walked to the door, saying under her breath, "Who would need me that urgently?"

When she pushed open the door, she didn't see anyone at the counter, and the night owls were gone. She looked over at Amanda, who pointed to the front of the café, where someone sat staring out the window. When she got a better look at the figure, her heart stopped. Silvery-blonde hair tied back in a small bun poking out of the back of a baseball cap.

Turning back to Amanda in order to dismiss her for the night, she saw that Amanda had already retreated to the kitchen. Bridgette tried to make herself look presentable by pushing her flyaway hairs back, brushing the crumbs and flour off as much as she could, knowing it wouldn't be enough. She reached into the glass display case to grab a croissant, plating it, and finally making her way over to the person who she hoped she was actually seeing.

When she got to the table, she placed the croissant down and the face turned upward.

"우 신." She exhaled in relief as if she had been holding her

breath, holding his name, since he walked out of her shop four months ago.

"안녕*, 누나." His smile was optimistic, and the most cheerful smile. His eyes danced with true happiness, and she knew. She knew he had gotten the help he needed. "오랜만이야†."

"우 신." She repeated his name to confirm she was seeing him correctly.

"네, 누나, 나야‡." He stood up, towering over her once again, pulling off the baseball cap to reveal the black roots of his hair that had started growing out. His face, while still chiseled, was fuller, sending a joyful thumping right to her soul.

She watched his face light up at her reaction to seeing him. Tears brimmed in her eyes as she saw the same in his. She jumped up to bring her arms around his neck; his went around her waist, lifting her in the air and spinning her around. Her legs wrapped around his waist, and she buried her face in his neck, taking in his scent. She needed to make one hundred percent sure he was truly there, with his arms around her.

He kissed the side of her head multiple times, and she settled into him. She pulled away from his neck and was face-to-face with him.

"I saw you were in town, but when I hadn't heard from you after you left that morning, I thought you had no interest in me. As a partner or otherwise." She pulled him closer again.

"I saved your number and had wanted to call and text you so many times. Thousands of times. It's embarrassing how often I thought about it." He laughed and she felt his chest bounce against hers. "But I wanted to be a better version of myself before I did that. You're the reason for that."

She unwrapped her legs from his waist, and he gently lowered her to the ground as she released her hold of his neck.

"나?"

---

* 안녕 – annyeong – hi (informal)

† 오랜만이야 - olaenman-iya – long time no see

‡ 나야 – naya – it's me

"네, 누나." He smiled as he cupped her cheek. "That night you opened up about your struggles, your worries, your insecurities. It made me face my realities as well. And when you asked if I was okay, I knew I wasn't. I'm pretty sure that's why you asked in the first place."

She reached up to cup his cheek as well.

"I knew I wasn't," he repeated, "but I also knew I would be. And it was all thanks to you."

"Oh 우신," she cooed as she leaned up to peck him on the lips. It didn't stay a peck for long. His hand went to the back of her neck, pulling her into him and kissing her like she was his oxygen. It was a different kind of kiss from the ones they shared four months ago. This one held hope for the future. A future together.

Their lips separated when they heard loud cheers coming from outside the café. Looking out, they saw a group similar to the drunkards that had started their story four months ago, only this group was watching them make out in an empty café and cheering them on.

They both laughed, and she buried her face in his chest out of embarrassment.

"We *could* give them a real show." His voice had gone deeper, and his hold on her hips pulled her into him, where she could feel his arousal. Her head left the safety of his chest and her eyes met his. There wasn't an ounce of humor in his voice or in his face. He was being dead serious.

"우신..." She had so many thoughts running through her mind. Amanda was still cleaning in the kitchen, there were people outside who could see his face and potentially recognize him and post what could be insanely compromising photos, which could get him immediately removed from CLAR1T.

Suddenly the lights in the café went out and they were plunged into near total darkness. The only light came from the streetlamps outside. And then she heard the door close in the kitchen—the door that led to the back entry and her apartment entrance. Before long Amanda came out from the alley onto the street and waved in the general direction of the building.

Right, the mirrored glass. They could see out, but people couldn't see in once the lights in the café were off. Her heart drummed so fast she was sure he could feel it beating against his chest. She could feel his as well.

"Lock the door," she instructed, and a glint of wild amusement spread across his face.

He cupped her cheek, her eyes shimmering with similar delight. "I did that the second I walked in."

Her breath caught and his smile got even wider.

"Have you been imagining this?" she teased while her hands roamed up and down his chest.

"Since I left the shop with you that night and saw the windows were mirrored." His hand on her neck, his thumb grazing her jaw— she was wet for him in an instant. She wanted him to do everything he was imagining.

He dipped his head down, his lips meeting hers again. She loved how they fit. Their bodies, their minds, their hearts. Everything melted together.

"I have something for you," he said on her lips.

"You are gift enough." She smiled, kissing him fervently.

"I promise you'll like this gift as well." He chuckled as he reached behind her to the table where a familiar backpack sat. He pulled something out of the large pocket. The second she saw it, she let out a small giggle.

His headphones.

"Oh, we don't need those anymore.' She blushed before making a rather brave confession. "Ever since our night together, I leave the window open when I try to relive that moment I had with you."

His mouth dropped open, his face becoming as bright red as hers, his eyes sparkling with lust and carnality.

"I'm jealous of everyone who got to hear those moans when I couldn't, 누나," he whispered. He put the headphones back down. "This can wait. But I can't wait any longer to be with you again. It was the most alive I've felt in years." He leaned down, his hands sliding down the sides of her thighs before gripping the inside of her knees and lifting her to once again have her wrapped around his waist.

She reached between them to unbutton and unzip his pants. He moved quickly so that by the time they had fallen to his ankles, he was dropping into one of the oversized leather chairs.

"How often have you thought about me?" he asked, putting his hands under her shirt to pull it over her head. "With your window open for others to hear you?"

She was kissing down his neck and pulling up his shirt so their heated skin touched like they had those months ago. His hand snaked up her neck into her hair, grabbing a handful and pulling up to get her eyes to meet his.

"말해 봐*," he commanded softly.

"Almost every day," she boldly admitted as she ground her hips down on his bare cock, wanting him inside her again. The growl he let out at hearing that made her shiver with desperation to be with him again.

"씨발." He made light work of unhooking her bra, and she unbuttoned her pants and got up from the chair, kicking off her shoes and dropping her pants. Before she could climb back on top of him, he got up from the chair, kicking off his own shoes and pants and pulling her toward him.

"I am going to give you even more to think about and touch yourself to until we meet again." He pulled her around to the back of the chair. "Hands on the chair."

She bent forward, grabbing the chair. It reminded her of their moment in the entryway to her apartment, and she could feel herself dripping with excitement.

He grabbed her ass and let out a moan. "You're already so wet for me, 누나. You've soaked your panties." His fingers played with the edges of her underwear. "I guess I shouldn't make you wait any longer."

His finger wrapped around the thin elastic strap at her hip and pulled hard with a loud snap; they fell to the ground between her

---

* 말해 봐 - malhae bwa – say it

spread legs. The sting was forgotten the second he entered her bare, filling her to the hilt. She didn't hold back her moan of pleasure.

"Oh 누나, look at you letting go, letting me hear your pleasure so freely." His hands went to her hips as he pulled out and pushed right back in, making her head fall. "Lift your head, 누나. I want you to watch people pass by as I make you beg for me to let you cum."

"우 신," she moaned out his name, following his orders to lift her head and stare out the window. What she didn't expect was to see a faint reflection of them in the window. "I-I can see us too."

"응. Do you enjoy that?" He continued his delicious rhythm of pumping inside her. She was on the balls of her feet, lifting herself up to meet his thrusts.

"네." She watched him in the window. His mouth hung open and she met his eyes in their reflection. She felt her walls clenching as he hit just the right spot, her arms starting to buckle and her head dropping.

"Keep your eyes on the windows. I want you to watch us. I want you to watch how much you enjoy the thrill of possibly being caught." He moved one of his hands up her torso and grabbed her breast, squeezing it, his finger rubbing the nipple into a hard peak before gripping it again.

"I want to really see your face," she admitted as she let go of the chair with one hand and held onto his hand squeezing her breast. "보고싶었어*."

His hips stuttered and suddenly he pulled out of her, a cold breeze running across her backside. She let go of the chair and turned to see him watching her, his eyes wide and glistening in the light from the streetlamp.

"Say it again," he begged. Her heart was full—it had been since he walked into her café four months ago. She wanted to make sure his heart was able to be full as well.

She pressed her naked body to his, wrapped her arms around his neck, and brought her lips to his ear, whispering, "보고싶었어."

---

* 보고싶었어 - bogosip-eoss-eo – I missed you

The smile on his face lit up her heart. Blood coursed through her veins at an alarming speed as he expressed such joy by her simple words. Before she could ask if he had missed her as well, he threw her over his shoulder and she let out a squeal. She playfully slapped his back so he would put her down.

He laid her down horizontally on the leather couch. It was somewhat sticky from her sweat, and as she tried to adjust herself, he grabbed one of the pillows and placed it under her, lifting her hips.

"나도 보고싶었어." He leaned down to grab her hands and put them to his lips and then on his chest. "너무 너무 보고싶었어."

"Please," she begged, wanting more of everything he was willing to give. "Please, show me how much."

Her hands, while still being gently held by him, scratched at his chest, and little red lines began to form instantaneously.

"I can show you more than just how much I missed you." Using one of his large hands to hold both of hers, he put them over her head and held them on the armrest. He leaned down to take one of her breasts in his mouth and she nearly launched off the couch. His mouth on her body was more intoxicating than she had remembered. It was like lightning striking, sending electric shocks through her whole body.

"I can show you how much I want you." He kissed down her body until his lips were so close to her most intimate spot. "Need you." He kissed her inner thighs, causing her to spread her legs wider. "Love you." He had let go of her hands, moving them down to her hips.

She was about to give in to her desire when the realization of what he had said came through the fog of lust. She grabbed onto his hair that was in the small bun at the back of his head and pulled his face back up.

"Wh-wh-what did you just say?" she wanted to believe she'd heard correctly, but her mind tried fighting that idea. It was a scenario she had played out in her head thousands of times. Maybe not the having sex on her café's couch aspect, but hearing him say he loved her.

"I said I love you. Which is probably the simplest way for me to say how my heart has been a mess since I left." He kissed her stomach and continued, "The number of times I thought about getting on a plane and flying to you is so high, it borders on infinity. I wondered, how were you doing? How was the café doing? Were the kids and their moms in the shelter able to enjoy your delicious food? Was the bar still serving you delicious beers?"

He left kisses on all the skin he could reach before lifting his head again. "I wondered, were you happy? Sad? Mad? Were you thinking about me as much as I thought about you?"

"우신." She cupped his cheeks to bring him back up her body, face-to-face with her. "I wondered about you all the time as well. I hoped you would be happy and would maybe think about me every now and then."

She watched his eyes light up again, and it was a million of Cupid's arrows straight to her heart.

"I love you too. And I hope you know I mean that not as a fan of you and your group, but as Bridgette." She stroked his eyebrows, watching his face relax and a smirk play on his lips.

"So you don't love CLAR1T anymore?" he teased, pinching her sides.

"I would *never* say that. I am in this CLARvoyant life for good," she kidded back as she laughed from ticklishness.

The playfulness died down and they were left with a comfortable heat between them. He leaned down, his lips softly meeting hers. His tongue swiped at her bottom lip and she gently opened her mouth, their tongues meeting in a playful dance. Her hands traced down his torso, which had become more muscular since they last met, all the way to his hard cock. When she wrapped her hand around it, he dipped his hips, the tip of his cock finding her entrance easily.

She arched her hips up, sliding more of him into her. When she released her hold, he plunged fully into her. She let out an excited shout as he filled her again.

"My beautiful 누나," he said, his lips never leaving hers. He reached between them, his fingers finding her clit remarkably quick, and she let out a loud moan. She saw the smile break out on his lips with her every whimper, and when his eyes met hers, the entire room warmed like there was a fierce fire burning around them, ready to consume them whole.

His hips ground into her at a satisfying leisurely pace but with a force that had her head inching closer and closer to the armrest. She reached behind his head, yanking out the elastic holding his hair back. She had loved watching it fall and frame his face the first time she had seen it freed, and she was desperate to stroke it and grip it tightly now, as they rode out their orgasms together.

"You really do take my cock so well. I love feeling you pulse around me, begging for your sweet release." His lips dropped to her neck, then his tongue traced down to her breasts, giving each nipple a flick and making them harden before moving back to her lips.

Two could play at that game, and she leaned up to flick his as well, tasting his sweat mixed with a cologne of buttery roasted coffee. It was delicious, and she wanted more of it. Her lips kissed as much of his chest as she could reach. He spluttered a moan and his hips jerked out of rhythm. That motivated her to keep going.

"If you keep that up, 누나"—his pace picked up speed—"I'm not going to be able to last much longer."

She didn't say anything, instead choosing to use her actions as her response. Her tongue traced up his chest, taking in that delicious flavor of his, before bringing her lips back to his. She lifted her hips higher than the pillow offered to make their bodies meet faster and with more strength.

"누나..." He was struggling to keep his composure, and that made her push further. Her hand went around the back of his neck, up into his hair, and gripped it firmly as she brought her lips to his ear.

"How about we count to three together?" she whispered before taking his earlobe between her teeth and nipping gently.

With that it was like he became an animal uncaged. His thrusts gained speed with a force she knew was going to leave her enjoyably sore the next morning.

"하나*," she moaned into his ear as his head dropped to her shoulder.

"둘†," he breathed before biting said shoulder with a loud growl.

"셋‡." She gripped his hair as his thrusts met her at a brutal pace. The sounds of their bodies meeting filled the whole café, and on that count of three, her mind went blank, her vision black, her body shivered, and her toes curled.

It took a few seconds for her vision to return, with little bits of light twinkling like fairy lights, but she was able to make out the face of the man she loved, looking down at her from an upright position with a satiated smile. His abs were on full display, his chest was heaving like hers, and he swallowed hard, her eyes following the bobbing of his Adam's apple.

"미안, do you have a towel?" He bent, and she saw his cock in his hand, cum dripping from the tip and covering her stomach. His fingers slowly pulled out of her dripping pussy. "I was in such a rush I forgot to put a condom on."

She pointed behind the counter. "There should be a pile of small cleaning cloths by the coffee machines."

He got up from the couch and made his way behind the counter. She enjoyed the view of his firm ass and, on his way back, his delicious abs. He brought the towel to her stomach, cleaning his cum off and causing her to laugh at how ticklish it felt. He smiled softly at her.

"Should we head upstairs for round two?" he joked.

"Why waste time going up there?" She grabbed his hand and pulled him back down onto the couch, knowing there were a lot more fun positions they needed to try before she had to be realistic and figure out a way to sanitize the couch for the next morning.

---

* 하나 – hana - one
† 둘 – dul - two
‡ 셋 – ses - three

CHAPTER TEN

"I wanted to ask, do you know someone who lives in the building next door named Sophia?" 우신 asked as his fingers traced up and down Bridgette's arm after their third round and what felt like her millionth orgasm of the night from their thousandth position on the couch.

"She's my best friend actually..." That was when it dawned on her that he had mentioned someone in her life she couldn't remember bringing up. Moving away from him to give his naked form a questioning up and down glare, she asked, "How do *you* know Sophia?"

He let out a loud laugh, grabbing for her to come back into his arms. "She never mentioned meeting a member of CLAR1T?"

"No, I know she is seeing one of your staff though. She had mentioned when you guys came here on tour that she hooked up with one of them and they decided to make it work. And I think it will because she is set to move to Seoul in two weeks to start teaching," she explained as she brushed her hand over his bare chest. She loved seeing how his body reacted to her touch.

"Technically he is staff. And by staff, I mean he's a group

member of CLAR1T." His chuckle caught her off guard. But not as off guard as his statement.

She flew off the couch this time and began grabbing for her clothes. "네?!"

"성준 followed me to the café." 우신 sat up, grabbing his pants from off the floor beside him. "I thought it was bizarre until I realized he wasn't following me, he was meeting his girlfriend. He pointed to where she lived, and it was the apartments right next door. "I wondered if you knew her."

"Finish getting dressed. We're going over there," she commanded.

"누나, it isn't that serious is it?" He pouted as he slowly followed her orders. "I only have a few more nights here. Why should we waste the precious time we have together?" He tried to stop her, but she was laser-focused on finding Sophia and 성준.

"가자*." She put her hand out for him to take, then pulled him out of the café to the building beside her business and residence.

Climbing up to the third floor, she was about to knock on the door when she heard banging from inside, followed by a moan.

"They're busy." 우신 grabbed the wrist of the hand he was holding and tried to get her to leave.

"야†!" she hollered as she banged on the door. Suddenly all the noise from the apartment stopped. She pounded on the door again. "야! Sophia, I know you're in there. And I know who you're with. Open the door now!"

The door flung open. Sophia's hair was everywhere, her lips were swollen, her makeup was smeared, and her sheets were wrapped around her body.

"Bridgette, what the— 어? 우신 씨?" Sophia saw the man behind Bridgette. Another hand landed on the door and pulled it open wider. A head popped out from behind, and Bridgette's eyes widened.

"Sophia, who is— 어? 우신 형?" 우신 hadn't been lying. 성준

---

* 가자 – gaja – let's go

† 야 – ya – Ya (it's to get someone's attention, but can be perceived as rude.)

pulled the door open more to reveal him shirtless in a pair of boxer briefs.

Bridgette was about to cover her eyes before her eyes were covered for her by 우신.

"Put your clothes on now." 우신 sounded pissed.

"침착해 형*." She heard 성준 say, and 우신 dropped his hand for Bridgette to still see Sophia, bright red standing at the door.

"You said he worked on the CLAR1T tour, not that he *was* the CLAR1T tour!" Bridgette wasn't upset about who her bestie was dating but the fact that she didn't trust her enough to tell her who she was in a relationship with.

"I'm kettle, nice to meet you, pot." Sophia put out her hand to Bridgette as she gave 우신 a once-over. "How are you doing, 우신 씨? 성준 mentioned you were going to the café downstairs. I didn't realize you two knew one another."

Sophia wasn't wrong, but at the same time she wasn't right. Prior to that night Bridgette and 우신 had only been together for one night, nothing more. Meanwhile for the last four months, Sophia was in a full-blown relationship with a member of the group, who Bridgette had thought was just a CLAR1T staff member. Sophia was moving to Korea for who knew how long to be a teacher so she could be with him. Bridgette knew there was no point in fighting nuance.

"We met the night of their last show in the city. We ran around town together and one thing led to another. It was only that one night. We didn't keep in touch. He then showed up tonight and asked if I knew a Sophia, then mentioned how 성준 was next door."

"잠깐만." 성준 reentered the doorway fully dressed. "This is the café girl who convinced you to get help?"

Bridgette froze. An arm wrapped around her neck gently, and she felt the weight of his head landing on her shoulder, putting him cheek to cheek with her. She felt the small nod of his head.

"She's the one you wrote the song about?" 성준 had spoken so

---

* 침착해 형 - chimchaghae hyeong – calm down bro.

matter-of-factly, but both she and Sophia stared at 우 신. Bridgette felt another nod on her shoulder.

Sophia then turned her gaze back to Bridgette. She didn't need to say anything. They had been friends long enough to know what the other was thinking. *Coffee. Tomorrow morning. HUGE debrief.*

With nods to one another, Sophia pulled 성준 away from the door, letting it close for them to continue their night. Bridgette was left with 우 신, who had a lot of explaining to do.

"Ready for those headphones now?" he whispered in her ear before nipping her earlobe gently.

우 신 BROUGHT BRIDGETTE BACK DOWN TO HER CAFÉ AND GRABBED the headphones off the table where he had tossed them. He could see in her eyes that she had a million questions running through her mind, but he knew once the headphones were on, she would have all the answers she wanted.

Slipping them over her ears, he pulled out his phone to bring up the demo of one of the songs that would be going on their next album. An album she had been the muse for. She was about to find out just how much of an impact she'd had on him.

Her mouth opened, about to ask a question, but he cut it off by hitting play. She froze as the music reached her ears, and he watched her begin to bop to the song. It was *her* song.

"카페 누나*…" she said louder than he believed she intended, since she couldn't hear herself. And once she spoke those words, her eyes went wide and her mouth opened and shut several times. "카페 누나?!"

He laughed at how shocked she was by hearing the phrase. He nodded and pointed to her as she continued to listen. She put her hands to the headphones as if that would make the music louder or to see if she was hearing his lyrics correctly. He knew she wasn't fluent in Korean, so he tried to put some of the most important

---

* 카페 누나 - kape nuna – café noona

parts in English. But he knew she would look up the translation once the song was released and she would see just how deeply he had fallen for her.

He checked his phone to see the song was coming to a close, and as it ended, she continued to hold the headphones to her ears. She was a statue. He was about to ask if she was okay when her gaze lifted to his. Slowly she peeled off the headphones and handed them back to him.

"That-th-that song…" She pointed to the phone and head-phones in his hands. "That song, you wrote it?"

"About you." He put the electronics down on the table and grabbed her hands. "I told you that you helped me that night we met. I was in a bad place, and you could tell. Scarily fast I think you knew I was in need of help. You treated me as any other person walking into your shop. And even when you realized who I was, you talked with me as me, 우신. Not 우신 of CLAR1T, the least liked —" He cut himself off before she could. He knew she hated his self-deprecation, and his therapist had also told him to put a stop to it. "미안. At the time I thought I was the least liked member of the group."

She let go of his hands to switch hers to the bottom and pull them to her lips, her eyes watering as he explained.

"That whole night, I was just me. I was allowed to be just me. That broke me loose of the fear of creating new music, the fear that I would never be able to produce again, the fear of asking for help. You freed me, Bridgette. My 카페 누나." He smiled as tears filled his eyes as well. "I hope this song shows you just how much you have meant to me since I met you."

"In the song you said…" She paused, trying to recall the lyrics. "그댄 내 전부니까, 카페 누나*."

"응…우와…한국어 실력이 많이 늘었어†," he said, impressed

---

* 그댄 내 전부니까, 카페 누나 - geudaen nae jeonbunikka, kape nuna – because you're my everything, café noona
† 우와…한국어 실력이 많이 늘었어 - uwa…hangug-eo sillyeog-i manh-i neul-eoss-eo – wow your Korean has improved a lot

with how well she spoke and how well she remembered the lyrics already.

"Everything?" She squeezed his hands even harder.

"응, 전부*." He smiled, dropping his head, his lips meeting hers. "I want everything with you. My future is with you."

"My whole life is here, 우 신. Yours is around the world." She began to sob. Tears streamed down his face. "Do you really see us working?"

"Couples make long distance work all the time. Why would we be any different? Sophia and 성준 are making it work for now. I think we can too." Tears fell from his eyes. It wouldn't be easy—their lives were different from his friend and hers.

"Since I met you, I've thought about you every day," he confessed.

"I've thought about you as well," she professed as well, which made his heart swell to nearly double in size.

"I've wanted to be with you every day," he continued, watching her mouth open and close before waiting for him to say something else. "Then let's try and make this work. 누나, I want to be with you however we can." He pulled her to him, but she continued to stare at him, not giving him a response. Her silence worried him.

But finally, she nodded. Tears in her eyes, she continued to nod.

"That's a yes, right?" He wanted to be one hundred percent positive before he lifted her into his arms.

"Yes." She laughed as more tears fell from her eyes, but he knew they were the same happy tears that were spilling from his own.

His arms enfolded her waist, and he lifted her into the air, spinning her around. He loved hearing her laugh as her arms wrapped around his neck and her hand stroked his hair.

He was happy. A feeling he had dreamed of feeling again. He was content. A concept he was worried he would never find on the road. He was inspired. A clearer head from his therapy sessions mixed with a café and its owner sparking that creativity. He was in love. A gorgeous woman who took the time to show him kindness,

---

* 응, 전부 – eung, jeonbu – yes, everything

care, and love, and whom he was able to hold in his arms again and planned to for a long time coming.

His 카페 누나.

EPILOGUE

Five years later…

        Bridgette stood with Sophia and the other CLAR1T members' girlfriends and fiancées on the side of the stage, as their boyfriends and fiancés performed their hearts out to a crowd of over twenty thousand CLARvoyants in the Seoul Arena. Nerves were getting to her, as once the concert ended she was going to give 우 신 some of the craziest, biggest, most exciting news she had to date.

The guys had all announced their relationships to non-celebrity women throughout the last five years. While there had been a huge uproar among the fandom—like demands for the members to be removed immediately (those fans didn't think that one through because that would mean there would be no more CLAR1T), as well as threats to their lives and the lives of their significant others—their management was very progressive in their mindset of how to handle these "scandals".

우 신 said it was because their company had been acquired right before CLAR1T had debuted. Although it had headquarters in Korea, it was a US-based company; the latest CEO, when she took over, had made changes to a lot of the legality revolving

93

around dating in the Korean music industry. She had even given a massively important speech about how she planned to tackle defamation lawsuits and disrespectful actions toward the idols and their partners.

Bridgette was very thankful for that. She had avoided social media for a while after 우신 announced he was in a relationship. While at first, he didn't mention her name or post anything about her, whenever he came to visit the US, fans noticed he would visit a certain city constantly. Some fans, more like the 사생 of the group, followed him one night, and soon their whole relationship became out in the open. Their exhibitionism in the bedroom came to a near halt after that.

But aside from that, Bridgette had started making yearly trips to Korea, killing two birds with one stone as she was able to see 우신 and her bestie, Sophia. She fell in love with the country rather quickly, having two people she loved the most living there. And she struggled a bit in the beginning when both her best friend and her boyfriend were so far away.

She'd known long distance was going to be hard and that their relationship would be harder than most. But they made it work. She would never deny she had her moments. Moments when she thought they wouldn't work out anymore, moments when they would fight about not seeing each other enough because of their jobs' hours, moments when she could see 우신 was struggling again and she wasn't able to hold him and help. That last one was probably the one that hurt her the most. But luckily, he continued to go to therapy, and once again his management began making strides in the right direction to support mental health within the K-pop business.

우신 told Bridgette that the reason he had come back to Korea after their first US tour was because the CEO had asked for him to be brought to her office to discuss his therapy and how to make it a topic idols shouldn't be afraid or ashamed of. She wanted her company to better itself in terms of how to handle the situation. He helped her to create a mandatory mental health exam every six months for not only the idols but everyone in the company, and if tests hit a certain level, that person would receive therapy through the company.

He had been able to openly talk about his struggles in interviews, which had resonated with so many fans that she saw him skyrocket into people's bias and no longer bias wrecker status. Bridgette always tried to share with him the praise of the CLARvoyants and even the media, so he knew how much he was loved.

The loud screams of the crowd and the lights going black on stage shot her back into the moment. In a few short minutes, she was going to give 우 신 a hopefully exciting surprise. All the boys came running off the stage and into the arms of their significant others.

우 신 wrapped his sweaty arms around her, and she gave him a big squeeze, taking in the smell of his hard work. He kissed her chastely and grabbed her hand for her to follow him back to the green room. Everyone was celebrating the performance the guys had put on, the energy of the crowd, and all their solo stages. Drinks were flowing, food was consumed, and the vibe in the room was full of happiness and love.

Slowly the other members began to leave with their partners until it was just Bridgette and 우 신. She had planned that with the girls, actually. They didn't know why exactly, but she hinted it would be helpful.

"우 신?" she nervously called.

He looked up from his phone with a bright smile. He'd been looking for a place to take her out after the show. "네, 누나?"

"I wanted to ask you a hypothetical question." She moved to sit on his lap from the couch beside him.

"This isn't one of those 'would I love you if you were a worm' questions, right?" he joked as he wrapped his arms around her waist and leaned back against the couch.

They both laughed and she shook her head. "No, no, nothing like that."

"Okay, I'm listening." He squeezed her waist a bit harder.

"How would you feel if I were to move here, to Korea?" she asked.

"I would love it!" he exclaimed, his hug getting even tighter. "But I know that isn't possible, 누나. I know that and I'm okay with it."

"What if it was possible?" She slid off his lap to make sure she could take in his reaction.

"If that really were the case, I would start cleaning out space in my apartment for all your things, because obviously you would be moving in with me." He smiled, his eyes drifting into a daydream-like stare. "Or we could find a new place that is perfect for the two of us. Maybe a dog. Or a cat. Maybe both."

He shook his head as if he was pushing the cute idea away. It upset her to believe that he truly thought it would never be a reality.

"That sounds nice." She leaned over and kissed him sweetly. He let out a loud sigh, and that was when she pulled out the papers from her back pocket to hand to him.

"이게 뭐야?*" He took the documents from her and unfolded them to reveal her big surprise. She watched his eyes scanning the papers, getting wider and wider as he read them. "누나, 이게 뭐야?!" he repeated.

"It's my café here in Seoul. I open in two weeks." She smiled.

"Wh-wha-bu-yo— Wait." He struggled to finish words and finally chose to take a deep breath, giving the papers another glance and then grasping her hands. "Are you saying that you're moving here?"

She nodded.

"But your shop back—"

"I am now co-owner with Amanda. I will have to go back every three months or so for business stuff, but she will be in charge of all the day-to-day. We've grown so much in the last five years, thanks to you"—she cupped his cheek—"and I'm sick of being so far away from you for such long periods of time. I would rather leave for a week now and then than only see you for a week now and then."

She kissed him more deeply, feeling a smile growing on his lips.

---

* 이게 뭐야? - ige mwoya? – what's this?

He wrapped his arms around her waist again, pulling her back into his arms.

"How long have you been working on this?" He ran his hands through her hair.

"For the last year and a half, between the visa, paperwork, permits, and everything else," she explained. "When I came to visit you and you were off doing your dance practices, recordings, therapy, and the like, I was running to the café, meeting with the contractors. Sophia helped as much as she could when I was away as well.".

"Why did you hide it from me?" he asked.

"I wanted it to be one hundred percent complete. I didn't want to tell you, and then all of a sudden something fell through, and I wasn't able to open the shop." She also didn't want him to worry about all the details of getting the shop ready when he already had so much on his plate.

"It looks amazing, Bridgette. When do I get to see it in person?" His smile spread from ear to ear.

"Tomorrow, when the name of the shop gets put on the glass." Her smile matched his.

"What's the name?"

"팬 카페*."

There was silence between them, and her heart raced. Her smile faltered until he grabbed her hand and stood up, pulling her with him and walking them out of the green room and back toward the arena area. When they got on stage, the place was empty. Not a soul in sight. Which was odd. Usually there would be people dismantling the stage, lights, putting away all the equipment, people sweeping up the confetti and clearing the seats. But there was no one.

He continued to pull her to a staircase that led under the stage. They passed through the metal beams and small lights until, in the distance, she saw twinkling fairy lights. As they got closer, she saw there was a massive bouquet of flowers surrounded by those

---

* 팬 카페 - paen kape – fan café

glowing lights. In the bouquet was a small banner that read 팬 카페 축하해!*

"우 신!" she exclaimed. "How?"

He grabbed the bouquet and handed it to her. "You got some mail sent to my apartment last month. I wasn't paying attention to who it was addressed to of course, and was surprised to see a permit."

She covered her face with her free hand. "Oh my God, I can't believe this! I have been stressing out about telling you and you already knew!"

"Look at the flowers, 누나." His voice was soft, but she could make out a wobble. Dropping her hand she followed his directions. There in the middle of the flowers was a small box. If her heart was racing before, it burst out of her chest now.

"I was trying to figure out how to do this for close to a year now." He removed the box from the flowers. "I had even talked to the guys about potentially going on a hiatus. But when I saw that piece of mail, I was about to hop on a plane and propose that day."

They both laughed as he popped open the small velvet box. A micro light inside lit up a gold band with a stunning single large oval lavender sapphire at the center. It shimmered in the bright light in the box.

"But clearly you were keeping it a secret for a reason. I followed you a few days ago and saw you print those papers out at your shop and had a feeling you would be telling me soon. I made up my mind that I would be proposing to you after the show tonight." He took the ring from its little velvet pillow and grabbed her hand. "I made the banner just in case today was the day you decided to tell me about the café."

Her face hurt from smiling so hard as tears fell, staining her cheeks. Her fingers twitched in anticipation.

"Bridgette, 누나, will you marry me?" he asked.

She nodded vigorously, and he slipped the gorgeous ring on her finger. She wrapped an arm around his neck and brought his lips

---

* 팬 카페 축하해! - paen kape chughahae! – Congratulations Fan Café!

down to hers. Their teeth clanked together for a second from their smiles being so wide, before their lips softened the blow and his arm encircled her waist, crushing the bouquet between them.

She pulled back slightly to save the bouquet.

"I should mention I was able to convince the staff to give us a few hours alone in the arena." He smirked. "Let's make the most of it."

Bridgette's head fell back in a happy fit of laughter before following through to take advantage of the empty arena as an ecstatic exhibitionistic, newly engaged couple. It only added to the excitement that she was about to open her second coffee shop, lovingly named 팬 카페.

WANT CLARıT MERCH?

https://ko-fi.com/koreanfromccntext/shop

ACKNOWLEDGMENTS

Here we are again. Wow, you guys really have changed my life. I want to first and always thank my incredible husband. The man who always encourages me and pushes me to keep following my dreams. And a new addition to the forever thankful clan, my baby boy. Mommy loves you and can't wait to see what your future dreams are! I love you both so much it's actually super gross.

To my parents, who continuously encourage me. My mom, my author bestie, and book event travel buddy, thanks for never actually reading my spicy books. I don't know if you would ever look at me the same way again.

To my author friends, Morrigan, Bridget, Chantal, Garnet, Lee, and a million more I know I'm forgetting, seeing your successes push me to continue on this crazy road of being an author. From bouncing ideas off you, to having writing sprints, I don't think this book would've been finished on time without you.

To all my old and new BETA readers whose comments made me laugh out loud, and whose helpful notes had me write a better story.

And to every single person who reads these books and begs to know when the next one is coming out, I wouldn't be here without you.

Thank you to absolutely everyone in my life. If I didn't mention you by name, I'm sorry but please know I love you just the same.

FOLLOW ME

Website: koreanfromcontext.com
Instagram: @koreanfromcontext
Threads: @koreanfromcontext
Tiktok: @samanthaannauthor
Buy Me A Kofi: https://ko-fi.com/koreanfromcontext

OTHER WORKS

Seoul Searching
Matching Set
An Afternoon In Monaco (available on Kofi)

The Idolized Series
HER ULT
FAN SERVICE
FAN CAFÉ
BOOK 4 – Coming Soon
BOOK 5 - tbd
BOOK 6 - tbd

NOTES

Printed in Dunstable, United Kingdom

71841373R00079